3/03-6x
1/04-7x

DISCARD

LAS VEGAS - CLARK COUNTY
LIBRARY DISTRICT
833 LAS VEGAS BLVD, N.
LAS VEGAS, NEVADA 89101

Darkness, Darkness

Forever Twilight
Book One

Peter Crowther

This special signed edition
is limited to 750 numbered copies.
This is number **204**.

Darkness, Darkness

*Forever Twilight
Book One*

Darkness, Darkness

Forever Twilight
Book One

Peter Crowther

CEMETERY DANCE PUBLICATIONS

Baltimore
❖ 2002 ❖

Signed Hardcover Edition   ISBN 1-58767-049-6

DARKNESS, DARKNESS
FOREVER TWILIGHT: BOOK ONE
Copyright © 2002 by Peter Crowther

Artwork Copyright © 2002 by Alan M. Clark

This book is a work of fiction. Names, characters, places, and incidents are either a product of the author's imagination or are used fictitiously. Any resemblance to actual events or locales or persons, living or dead, is entirely coincidental.

All Rights Reserved.

Manufactured in the United States of America.

FIRST EDITION

Cemetery Dance Publications
P.O. Box 943
Abingdon, Maryland 21009
E-mail: cdancepub@aol.com

www.cemeterydance.com

The night has a thousand eyes,
And the day but one.
>   F. W. Bourdillon
>   *Among The Flowers*

We like to think we live in daylight,
but half the world is always dark;
and fantasy, like poetry,
speaks the language of the night.
>   Ursula K. LeGuin
>   Interviewed in *World Magazine*

Darkness, darkness
Be my pillow
Take my head and let me sleep...
In the coolness of your shadow,
In the silence of your deep.
>   The Youngbloods
>   *Darkness Darkness*

Prologue

It was always the same.

Rick was sitting in the car, reaching into the glove compartment in the dash to pull out a pack of *Juicy Fruit*, feeling his fingers touch the paper, a long, torn-off strip of yellow — even though, in the dream he could not experience the feeling of touching things and the dim light inside the glove compartment of the old DeSoto didn't permit the luxury of color definition — taking his eyes off the road, just for a second, taking his eyes away from the snow-streaked slopes of the Bighorn Mountains straddling the horizon, with I-90 snaking its way right for them, Lovell somewhere up ahead, over west, and Ranchester sitting way behind him, hearing the little voice in the back of his head, the one he used to talk to himself, hearing himself have it tell him

hey, the road...better keep your eyes on the road, dog-breath

he shouldn't let his attention drift, feeling a little tired (which was why he'd thought of the *Juicy Fruit*), thinking maybe he should roll down the window, let in a little air, seeing it all again, knowing that it was a dream and that he only ever thought all those thoughts the once, just the one time, and that this time was like he was playing a part, making the same moves all over again, even though he knew these were the wrong moves to make, then, calm somehow, calm inside of himself even though it was all going to happen again, seeing the guy being chased out of a wide parking area on the side of the road by a girl in cut-off blue denim shorts, the two of them laughing, then seeing *them* see *him*, watching their faces slide down on themselves like candle wax flash-fried, their smiling mouths first drooping at the corners and then their eyes widening, catching out of his eye corner the two bicycles propped against a pile of logs, Thermos beside them, and some kind of plastic carton, and all the time Rick bracing himself, his arms locked out holding the steering wheel, the yellow *Juicy Fruit* pack dropped to the floor beneath his feet, forgotten but

so, just how much value d' you place on a stick of gum, huh, Rick?

remembered in the dream, then slamming his feet on the pedals, nearly standing up on them, his backside off the DeSoto's seat, feeling the wheels lock, talking to himself

shitshitshitshitsh—

and being distantly aware of the dust clouds billowing at the sides of the car, seeing the faces of the guy and the girl

she had freckles, didn't she Rick? you remember that, don'tcha...you remember seeing her face in that much detail just before

before the car drove through them, the two of them first doubling over towards him, folding over the hood, the guy reaching out at the last minute to push the girl (it was his fiancée, Rick found out later...much later), and the girl disappearing somewhere — one minute there, the next minute gone — and the guy coming up over the hood, smacking down onto it and then up against the windshield and then, rolling and tumbling, up over the roof, hearing his body bouncing along its length while Rick felt the tell-tale judder of the DeSoto's tires going over something in the road, then looking in the rear-view, even as the car was finally slowing down, and seeing the guy's body falling onto the road like a rag doll

a very red *rag doll, huh, Rick?*

with another shape lying behind it a few yards back, and then the car coming to a halt and the engine cutting out and there being no sound at all, just Rick staring at that rear-view willing the two unmoving rag dolls to get to their feet, dust themselves down and give him the bird

hey, asshole, whyn't you come back and finish the job... think there's a couple of bones here seem to be still in one piece

but Rick knew the rag dolls would not move and he knew that the worst part of the dream was now waiting for him, crouched down like a feral cat behind a creaking cellar door, daring him to peer around and sneak a glance into the darkness: now was the part where he got out, hearing the soft clicks of the DeSoto's engine cooling down and the creak of the suspension as he swung his legs out onto the dusty road and pulled himself up to his full six-two, smelling the scorched smell of brake linings mixed with the cool fresh air blowing down from the mountains, glancing across to the pull-in and seeing the bicycles and the Thermos *hey, come on, quit fooling around now...coffee's getting cold*

feeling the sudden need to pee but, instead, forcing his legs — these two wobbly tentacles that didn't seem to have a single bone between them — to carry him back along I-90 towards the two shapes lying in the still-swirling dust, neither of them moving, knowing deep down that they wouldn't move just as they hadn't moved when it had first happened and they didn't move any of the other times, the reprise-times — like now — when they had to go through the whole thing again in Rick's dreams, knowing all this but, as each step brought them closer, straining to see a sign of movement, a sign of—

Someone shouted out and a light burned into his brain. Then it was gone.

One

Rick opened his eyes, suddenly aware in that instant that he had been dreaming again — the same old dream — and that he had shouted out. He looked around the porch and listened: it was silent. He listened again. No, it wasn't just silent it was...empty — no insect noises, no distant hum of an occasional late-night traveler negotiating the twists and turns of the highway down below.

There was a dull *crump* noise from somewhere outside, somewhere way off, out on the road. Then the silence returned.

As though in response, a burst of applause exploded from behind and Rick suddenly remembered he'd left the TV on.

"What the hell time is it?" he asked the night. No answer. It had to be before six a.m. which was when his show started — there was no way Geoff would let him sleep through that.

He bent down and lifted the bourbon bottle and the glass from the wooden deck, set them on the table alongside the lounge-chair he'd been stretched out in. As he considered one last swift shot before he went inside to bed he gave a mental vote of thanks to all-day and all-night TV. There was always something on and even though he had not been watching it, the sound was reassuring when he sat out on the deck staring over to the forest-clad hills in the distance, listening, as he did most nights, to the sound of the canned laughter on one of the sit-coms while he waited for the sun to drop down out of sight.

As he made to go inside he heard a muffled explosion.

When he turned back, he could see a fire on the road across the fields. It was a vehicle of some kind, a truck maybe.

Rick went inside.

Two

The light had come around four hours into the *Songs For Sleepers* section that ran from one a.m. until six. The show was a mixture of mood music, Melanie Grisham's sultry voice-overs and intros, and occasional phoned-in calls from folks either unable or unwilling to sleep...for whatever reason.

Some of them might be nursing bad relationships, some might be holding down night-shift jobs at the packing plant over at Carlisle, across the hills, or the trucking depot down at Dawson or even propping up the counter at Martha McNeil's Diner down the road in Jesman's Bend — affectionately known locally as the one-horse town to end them all ("...and even that one is lame," was how Rick usually ended those discussions). And one or two of them had some kind of psychological disorder, but Melanie didn't mind that. She reckoned they posed less of a problem to the world phoning her in the middle of the night — telling her they wanted to get into her pants and asking her about her pussy (Melanie's 15-second tape delay always kept such remarks off the air but she always managed to tell them she didn't own a cat) — than if they were out there roaming the streets, drinking their cocktails of oblivion and strength out of brown paper bags and talking to the moon...unless someone happened along they could talk to instead, someone who would be better off home and wrapped up in bed.

The light flashed and then disappeared. Just like that.

At a little after 5:15, the whole world had turned white, just for an instant, and then everything had gone back to normal.

Melanie was cueing up a CD of Perry Como's greatest hits — her mother's favorite — flicking forward to track 11, 'Magic Moments', when, suddenly everything in front of her had turned white. It wasn't just a glare from outside — like the headlights of an approaching car washing across the windows...except there weren't any windows connecting to the outside world in the studio — it was everything in the room, including the air itself: all definition had disappeared, a momentary white blindness, and then back the way it had been just seconds before.

"Jesus Christ!" Melanie hissed, yanking her hand back from the track button on the CD rig like the rig was a hot stove and she'd just touched it. "What the hell was that?"

Geoff rushed out of the sound booth and stood in the center of the room, looking around at the equipment, a copy of *Men's Journal* hanging from his hand. "You okay?" he asked when he was satisfied that nothing had blown.

Melanie nodded. The Sinatra song was coming to an end. She waved Geoff quiet and pulled the mic boom across to her. "Yeah, nobody told those stories like Old Blue Eyes," she said into the gauze, her voice smoky and just the right side of hoarse. She pressed the play button on the CD player. "We're gonna leap right on now with one of my mother's favorites. I'll be back to talk to you after this...a few 'Magic Moments' from Mr. Perry Como." As the first orchestral strains cut in, Melanie said, "And anyone out there needs someone to talk to in these lonely hours, just give me a call — you know the number." She pushed the boom away and wound up the volume.

She leaned back on her chair and held her hands straight out in front of her. They were shaking. She looked across at her husband and took a deep breath. "What was it?"

Geoff shrugged. "Nothing in here, that's for sure."

He ran a hand through his thatch of sandy hair and breathed deeply.

"So where was it, if it wasn't in here?" Melanie pointed across to the wood-paneled sidings that went all around the room. "Can't even see outside."

Rick appeared in the sound booth and started waving. Geoff waved him to come inside.

"There's a car, truck maybe, out on the forest road," Rick said as he came into the studio. "On fire."

"That must've been it," Geoff said. "Don't see how we could see it in here, though."

Rick looked from Geoff's face to Melanie's. "That must've been what?"

Melanie shook a Marlboro from a pack on the console and lit it. "Some kind of light," she said, blowing out smoke in a thin stream, watching it curl up below the light. She placed the cigarette on the lip of a Coca Cola ashtray and flicked through a CD rack.

Rick frowned and thought back to sitting out there on the deck at the back of the station, remembered the dream and waking up from it. "No, the light came first."

Geoff walked across and shook himself a cigarette out of Melanie's pack. "Before the truck?"

"I don't know for sure it's a truck. Could be a car. But it's burning."

Melanie seemed to have found what she was looking for. She flipped open a CD case and slipped the CD into the second player, cueing a particular track. "You boys want to talk about it in the booth? I've got a show to do."

They walked out and secured the studio door.

"I think we need to go out, take a look," Rick said, watching his brother flop onto the sofa. "Could be somebody's hurt."

"Uh uh. I'll call Eddie at the station. Let *them* go." He blew out smoke and adjusted himself, fought back a yawn. "You say it was on the forest road?"

Rick nodded.

"Mm hmm, could be they're even nearer than we are." He reached over to the desk and lifted the phone, keying in the number with his other hand.

"Many calls?"

Geoff shook his head, listening to the *brrrt brrrt* in the earpiece. "Never are around this time. Folks are all curled up doing what they should be doing—"

"Or what they *shouldn't* be doing!" Rick added with a big smile.

"And it's a big Amen to *that* one," Geoff said returning the grin. "Leastwise, they ain't wanting to talk to folks over to the radio station, and that's a fact."

Rick leaned against Geoff's desk and scanned the walls, taking in the posters and the Vargas calendar months — there were 27 of them, some of them more than 30 years old. He smiled and shook his head. "Mel ever say anything about those?"

"The Vargas girls?"

"Uh huh."

"Why would she say anything?"

Rick gave a little shrug. "Like maybe she thinks they're a little tacky."

"Tacky!" Geoff snorted. "They're art. Ain't nobody ever drew a woman like Vargas." He slammed the phone down on the cradle and picked it up again, re-keyed the numbers.

"Busy?"

Geoff shook his head and slouched back against the cushions, the phone at his ear again. "No answer."

"Who's on tonight?"

"Eddie — Eddie for sure — Shirley maybe? Don... Troy?"

"Didn't Barbara deliver yet?"

Geoff shrugged.

"I think she did. A girl, as I recall. Janey told me, over to the deli? It's my guess Troy will be home nights for a couple weeks."

"Well, maybe." Geoff stubbed his butt out in a saucer on the sofa's arm. "Still should be somebody picking up calls, though."

"Geoff, I think we should maybe go out there ourselves. Right now."

Geoff put the phone back on the cradle. He frowned up at his younger brother. He tried to see himself in Rick's face but couldn't. Rick was taller — six-two, a good three inches — with dark, almost black hair and a swarthy complexion. Geoff, meanwhile, was light-skinned — always a problem in the height of summer — and maybe a little on the stocky side.

"What about Mel?" he asked. "Leaving her here all alone?"

Rick waved his arms expansively. "I'll wake Johnny."

Geoff snorted. "He'll be so thrilled."

"Has to be done."

"You enjoy making him pissed. You know that, don't you?"

"Like I say, has to be done."

"But you *do* enjoy it."

Rick nodded and smiled. "Okay, okay...I enjoy it."

As Rick left the sound booth, chuckling, Geoff's own laughter died away and he glanced in at his wife. And then at the telephone.

Three

"You wanna die, right?" Johnny spoke without opening his eyes, his head almost completely buried face down in his pillow. "Whoever you are, you got bored with life and decided you wanted to try dying."

Rick removed his hand from John Meshtik's bare shoulder and sat gently on the side of the bed. "Johnny, you have to get up."

"Who says?" Still no movement.

"I say, Geoff says."

Johnny smacked his lips again and turned around. He shielded his eyes with his hands and looked up at Rick, squinting at the light from the hallway over his shoulder. "And why is that?"

"There's been an accident, out on the forest road, and we're—"

"What kind of accident?"

Rick shrugged and pushed the door closed, returning the room to gloom.

Johnny turned around and opened his eyes so they were slits. "Ah, thanks — that's better. What kind of accident?"

"Don't know till we get over there. Truck maybe, on fire."

"You call the Sheriff's office?"

Rick nodded. "Geoff did. No answer."

"No answer?" Johnny sat up in bed and lifted his watch from the side table. "It's after 5:30 in the damned morning. What could they be doing down there at this time?"

"Lines could be down," Rick said and then realized that that couldn't be true. He had heard the phone ringing when Geoff had dialed.

"And why would the lines be down?"

"Jesus Christ, Johnny, just get out of the fucking bed. We're going down to see if someone needs help."

"Okay, okay." Johnny pulled the sheets back and swung his legs out, yawning. "But why would the lines be down? There a storm?"

"Uh uh." Rick got up and opened the door again. "There was some kind of...some kind of light. Just before the truck crashed. If it is a truck...and if it did crash."

"If it didn't crash, why is it on fire?" Rick glared and Johnny sniggered, holding his hands up. "I'm getting out of bed, see? This is me—" he got to his feet and adjusted the waistband of his shorts "—getting out of bed, okay?"

"Okay."

He pulled a pair of jogging pants from the bureau behind the door and stepped into them. Then he slipped an already-buttoned creased shirt over his head and gave a mock bow. "Johnny is ready."

"I'm pleased."

They walked out into the hallway and made for the stairs down to the studio floor and the outside doors.

"You said there was a light?"

"Yeah, like a flash — lightning. Everything went white for a few seconds, then came back to normal."

"Sounds like we're gonna get a bitch of a storm." Johnny took hold of the handle into the studio and stopped. "You guys take it easy out there."

Rick nodded. "Look after Mel."

Johnny's eyes opened wide. "Hey, that's right. It's just me and the Lady Melvin...maybe she needs me to look after her, keep her warm against the nasty storm."

"Yeah, in your dreams."

When Rick stepped outside, his brother was already pulling the Dodge around the front of the building. Rick looked across the sweep of the valley to the forest road and saw the smoke. It didn't look as bad as it had before, but maybe that was because the first rays of morning sun were showing behind the hills, turning everything lighter... making everything seem less hostile, less mysterious.

Geoff leaned over and flicked up the door catch. "Get in," he said.

They drove in silence.

The sky behind the hills was lightening and by the time they had reached the vehicle — a flat-backed pick-up they knew was owned by Jerry Borgesson — shadows were already showing themselves.

"Jerry's truck," Geoff said as they pulled in behind it.

Rick didn't say anything.

The truck was plowed into the bushes at the right-hand side of the road. If it had drifted to the left, it would have gone over the side and straight down the steep wooded incline to the valley bottom. Rick looked across at Honeydew Mountain and saw the radio station straddling the flat middle section below the horned crown, tried to imagine Melanie speaking in husky tones into the mic, holding her early morning audience in raptures.

Geoff had moved around to the driver's door and his voice interrupted Rick's reverie. "He's not here," Geoff shouted. "Nobody's inside."

The fire had not done much damage although smoke was still fuming out from the buckled sides of the hood. Geoff reached in and switched off the ignition and the thin, watery headlights disappeared. Rick walked around the other side of the truck and looked inside the cab. It was empty, as Geoff had said. He opened the door and climbed inside.

"Can't get this side open," Geoff said through clenched teeth as he pulled at the handle. "Must've been damaged in the crash."

"There's nothing in here," Rick said. He was looking specifically for blood or a damaged dashboard or windshield to indicate Jerry Borgesson's bulk or head slamming into it. But the interior looked as good as new...or, at least, as good as fifteen years old would allow. There was a creased Polaroid of Jerry's wife, Shirley, slotted behind the rear mirror fixing plate, a half-eaten pack of mints lying on the plastic shelf housing the speedo, and a confusion of crumpled paper bags, breadcrumbs and apple and pear cores around the pedals. All pretty much the way Jerry's truck should be. Except for the fact that there was no Jerry.

Geoff moved back from the door, hands on hips, and turned around. He shouted Jerry's name and waited.

"You think he's hurt? Crawled off somewhere, maybe, to get away from the fire?"

"Something like that," came the reply. Geoff shouted again.

Silence reigned.

"Hey, Rick? You notice anything?"

Rick moved across to the driver's seat and rolled down the window. Leaning on the sill, he said, "Like what?"

Geoff turned around and looked at him and then glanced quickly away, as though what he was thinking was too preposterous even to verbalize it. "There's no sound," he said.

Rick leaned further out of the window and listened. Geoff was right. The entire valley was as still and as silent as a grave. No bird sounds. He sat back and shuffled around in the seat so that he was facing forward. He took hold of the steering wheel gingerly, allowing his hands to acclimatize themselves around the worn leather and the smoothed finger sections, fighting back the images of the young man and woman whose faces had stared at him as he ran them down. It was almost six months ago now but it still felt like yesterday.

He had sold the DeSoto to a dealer over in Carlisle, and though Geoff had reasoned with Rick that it wasn't Rick's fault and that it was just an accident...could happen to anybody, Rick wasn't having any of it. Now, all this time later, the feelings were not getting any better — if anything, they were getting worse, with the dream coming to him every night now instead of every few nights the way it had done immediately after the accident.

Rick looked across at the passenger door. "Geoff?"

"Yeah? You find something?" Geoff was kicking through the undergrowth at the side of the road above the incline.

"I just realized something."

"Yeah? What?"

"I opened the door." He turned to look at Geoff. "I opened the door to get inside here."

"And?"

"Well, if Jerry was hurt — or even just dazed — why would he close the door after him?" Rick pretended to stagger out of the cab and then turned to close the door. "Why would he do that?"

Geoff shrugged. "Truck-proud? Hey, I don't know."

"Doesn't make any sense. Doesn't make any sense him not turning off the ignition, either...particularly with the engine on fire." Rick removed his hands from the steering wheel and rubbed them down his trousers. They were clammy.

"He's probably lying somewhere out in the bushes," Geoff suggested, though the suggestion didn't sound all that convincing. "Or maybe—" he turned around with a big smile on his face "—maybe he walked into town! Yeah, that's it. That's what he's done. He's walked into town." He clapped his hands together. "He's walked into town because there's nothing else for him to *do* at five o'clock in the morning. Come on, let's drive on."

Getting out of the cab of Jerry's flatback pick-up was a huge relief for Rick though he didn't know whether that relief was simply a throwback to memories of the accident or something else. Something else entirely.

Four

The two or three miles down into Jesman's Bend were as silent as the valley had been just minutes earlier.

The initial euphoria of Geoff's solution that Jerry had walked into town was eroded almost as soon as they were back in Geoff's Dodge. The reason, quite simply, was the radio. They picked up KMRT okay, heard Melanie introduce Andy Williams singing 'Can't Take My Eyes Off You', smiled at each other

yep, everything is just fine...

and then Rick went and spoiled it all by turning the tuning dial.

He couldn't have put into words why he turned the goddamned dial but he did it. And

nope, everything isn't just fine...everything isn't just fine at all...

all they could pick up was static.

"Maybe it's some kind of massive electrical charge," Rick ventured. "Blown out—" he waved his arms like a huge flower opening its petals "—I dunno...blown out all the transmitters or something."

He looked across at Geoff and saw his brother raise his eyebrows.

"And," Rick continued, "we can only pick up Mel because we're so close to our own transmitter."

Then, turning out of the curve alongside Frank and Eleanor Dawson's house into Main Street, they saw the blue-and-white wrapped around the fire hydrant.

"I don't think so," Geoff said, his voice suddenly sounding tired. "I don't think it's that simple."

Geoff slowed down as they went by the car. It was Don Patterson's, easily recognized by the furry tail on the radio antenna. Most times either of them saw that furry tail, they had to smile. But this time, it just didn't seem funny. This time it seemed awfully sad. Almost pitiful.

"No point in getting out," Rick said.

"Uh uh. Car's empty."

"Maybe..." Rick started to say something, suggest some way that such things could happen in their town that would make everything seem right...but he gave up after just the one word and closed his mouth tight. There was no maybe about it. Something was awfully wrong.

Further along Main Street, Martha McNeil's Diner was ablaze with interior lights. Geoff pulled the Dodge into the sidewalk, parked it between an old Chevy two-tone that was more rust than paint and a little continental job with a floor-shift and a rear-mounted engine, and they got out.

The street was more than silent: it was like a canvas before the paint got put onto it. Empty, devoid of life, instead of just sleeping.

"You know," Geoff said, placing his hand on the hood of the Chevy like he was seeing if the engine was still warm, "why do I feel that we're not going to find anyone here in town?"

Rick's face was pressed up against the Diner window, looking past his own reflection into the strip-neon-lit interior, staring at the littered counter, the plates of half-eaten food, mugs of coffee, pieces of cutlery lying some on the plate, some on the counter and one or two on the floor behind the foot rail. He shifted to one side so he could get a look into the back, where Martha herself did the cooking, best plates of pancakes and flapjacks in the State. The kitchen was deserted.

"Where'd they go?" Rick said stepping away from the window and out onto the street. He didn't expect an answer and wasn't disappointed when he didn't get one.

"You think maybe it was some kind of radiation?" Geoff turned around and looked at his brother. "I'm just grasping at things here, you understand."

"Hey, grasp away."

"Well, like maybe the military came in and evacuated everybody."

"Including Don from his smashed up car? Jerry from his pick-up? And how come they didn't come for *us*? How come nobody even called us up and *told* us?"

He turned around, hands on hips, and shook his head. "And how'd they do it so fast? And—" He pointed down the street away from the stores, where the houses sprouted picket fences and grass so close-cut you'd have thought it had been trimmed using scissors. "Nobody leaving their door open. We knock on those doors, there's gonna be no reply. So, if they all just high-tailed it out of here with the military, in such a dad-burned rush, how come everyone remembered to close their door?"

"We don't know for sure that—"

Rick stepped onto the sidewalk, his shadow disappearing into the broadening shadow of the Diner's roof. "So let's find out."

"Rick..."

"Yeah?"

Geoff looked at his kid brother's face, studied the eyes and, in them, saw the same fears and uncertainty that sprawled in his own heart. Rick was bigger than him but Geoff always felt the need to take care of his kid brother. "It'll be okay," he said, and winked.

They stepped inside the Diner, listening for sounds and hearing nothing.

Five

All that was needed to complete the effect was an occasional tumbleweed blowing across Main Street and maybe the wind whistling around the saloon swing doors. But there were no saloon swing doors in Jesman's Bend.

In fact, there was nothing there at all...at least nothing alive.

Martha McNeil's Diner had been as silent as the grave. Plates of food half-eaten, mugs half full of coffee — now cool to the touch — a jacket slung over one of the booth stools (Jim Ferumern's, his wallet still in his pocket: forty-six dollars in bills plus a picture of his wife, Jacqui, and the two boys — Geoff didn't remember their names, if he'd ever known them — and a bunch of coins that slipped out of a side pocket and clattered to Martha's linoleum floor), and a magazine lying open on the counter beside a half cup of coffee and a Danish with a bite out of it...*Book*, open at a spread about a bookstore in New York, 'The Mysterious Bookshop'. Turning the magazine over to look at the cover, Rick dropped crumbs onto the counter from the open spread...the kind of crumbs that made him mad when he was reading: crumbs on the magazine — he always knocked them off or took more care eating.

Further down the street, houses were empty and silent. Knocks on doors and names called out by Geoff and Rick brought no response. Not even from Luke Napier's terrier, gone from the lavishly-built dog kennel by the front of the house...with its restraining chain lying curled up in a tangle alongside a bowl bearing the word 'Duffy' in scrawled paint.

Most of the doors were still locked against the night, even though by now, with all their looking and checking, it was almost eight o'clock. Those that were not locked, opened into silent homes, some of them with TV sets playing — some showing old movies and sitcom re-runs but some (the ones tuned into stations showing live material, Geoff guessed) showing static, and radios mostly playing the same...though on one or two they heard Melanie's smoky voice announcing a new song. They felt like thieves, stealing into the sanctity of friends' houses, breathing their air, smelling the smells of their homes. When they spoke they spoke in whispers, eyes pulled wide open in an effort to strengthen their hearing that they might discern even the tiniest movement, the laziest turn-over in bed. But the beds, when they found them, were like everywhere and everything else: empty, the sheets on many of them bunched up as though wrapped around slumbering figures that had suddenly blinked out of existence, pillows indented beneath non-existent heads.

The lights in the gas station glared dimly against the strengthening sunlight but Gram Kramer was nowhere to be found...though his prized leather jacket hung stiffly by the side of his stool in the windowed booth overlooking the pumps, a copy of the *Enquirer* open on the counter and a burned away cigarette butt sitting on the counter, a long perfectly formed funnel of undisturbed ash lying in the ashtray beside it. At least here there was some sense of normality — the radio was tuned into their station and Melanie's voice suddenly drifted in on the closing strains of Ray Charles's 'I Got A Woman', speaking to all those people who had loved ones "way over town". Her voice now had a sense of urgency, a sense of needing somebody to respond to what she was saying. Rick wondered what Mel and Johnny had been talking about up there on the mountain; wondered whether they'd started making telephone calls and finding nobody home. Nobody home anywhere.

"You need to give her a call," Rick said without turning.

"Uh huh," Geoff said. "I'll do it from Eddie's."

There were two blue-and-whites parked outside the Sheriff's office, which meant that there should be somebody inside. Even without the cars, there was no way Shirley Pakard would leave the office unattended. And how come nobody had wondered why they couldn't get a response from Don Patterson, his car wrapped around the fire hydrant on the outskirts of town? The answer was there was nobody to make that call, nobody to wonder why the response didn't come in.

Rick strode up to the door and pushed it wide.

"Troy, Shirley?"

Only a little over one hour ago, Rick and Geoff had edged into places shouting out names and other things to go with the names — things like, "Hey, what's happening?"

and "Come on, time to rise and shine" — but they had given that up after a while. Now they just burst into homes and through doors and even the shouted names were half-hearted at best, the volume of the call lessening each time.

Rick pulled a notebook from his jacket pocket and slumped into Shirley's chair. He pulled the phone across the desk and started to dial.

"Who you calling?"

Rick leaned back and looked up at his brother. "Mom."

Geoff looked at his watch, about to say something — something like *don't call her yet, too early* or *let's not worry her about this...there has to be a logical explanation* — but he knew those would just be excuses. The fact was he feared the same thing that his brother feared, though neither of them was prepared to put it into words. He leaned against the desk and waited.

When Angela Grisham's voice came on the phone, Rick's face lit up like a fourth of July fireworks display... but when that voice kept on talking without waiting to hear what Rick had to say — telling him she couldn't get to the phone right now but instructing him (even though the long-ago recorded voice didn't know who she was talking to) to leave a message — his face collapsed. He returned the phone to the cradle. "It's eight o'clock — she should be there. Whatever it is, it stretches out to the west coast."

Geoff said, "Try Mel's brother, Bob...New York." He recited the 212 number from heart and watched Rick prod the keypad.

"What time is it there?" Rick said as he listened to the ringing tones.

Geoff checked his watch. "Around eleven. He should be there." Bob and Linda McAuley worked from home, running a small press publishing operation in the Village. They were always there, at least one of them. But not today.

Rick shook his head. "No answer."

Whatever it was, it stretched right across the country.

They didn't like to think how much further it went.

"You gonna call Mel?"

Geoff shook his head. "Let's just get back to the station," he said.

Six

They didn't go back to the station, not right away. Geoff had second thoughts and headed the Dodge out of Jesman's Bend the eighteen miles to Dawson. But it was a wasted effort.

They heard the horn plaintively wailing long before they had passed the tracks on the town outskirts, its drone hanging on the wind like a half-remembered tune or the tired buzzing of a wasp trapped against the window-pane in a deserted room.

The cause was an old Lincoln, all chrome and fins, its front end sitting in the double-fronted window of a deli on Milton, where the street curved slightly to the intersection with Boedeckers. They didn't stop to look, but as they passed the Lincoln, driving slowly, praying silently for any movement, Rick wondered whose car it was and why he or she was out so early in the morning. It was almost nine by that time but they both assumed the smash-up happened in the early hours, same time as the light.

A little further along, another car and a delivery truck had met head on at the intersection. The car was a wreck and the delivery truck had jack-knifed onto its side so that it was spread right across the road. A few yards beyond, they saw a bicycle lying by the side of the road, a burlap sack of spewed-out newspapers littering the sidewalk. If they wanted to go any further they would have to park and proceed on foot. Without saying anything, Geoff slowed down and made a turn back the way they had come, back past the smashed Lincoln with its horn still wailing like an abandoned child — and, just like such a child who had been crying for attention for a long time, the horn's voice was growing hoarse.

Going back, they passed more empty streets and empty houses, with the only sign of movement being the flag over the courthouse, flapping in the wind.

They hit Jesman's Bend for the second time at a little before midday, pulling up outside the station ten minutes later. The sun was high and the shadows long. Neither of them was looking forward to the darkness, though they couldn't explain why.

This time they didn't stop.

Melanie was sitting on the rail outside the station's front entrance, coffee cup in one hand and cigarette in the other, its smoke drifting peacefully up into the air as though everything was absolutely normal.

"We're on strike," she announced as Geoff stepped out of the Dodge.

He nodded.

Rick walked up to her and tousled her thatch of blonde hair, closing his eyes and breathing in the smoke. "My, but that smells good."

Melanie squinted into the sun and gave a sorry-looking smile to her husband. "There's nobody there, is there?"

Geoff shook his head. "How did you know that?"

Melanie shrugged, took a pull on the cigarette. "No calls, no movement out on the road, no answer from people *we* called — some of Johnny's friends, my brother—"

"Yeah, I called Bob, too." Geoff stretched his arms behind his head and arched his back. "He could be out."

"Hey, don't bullshit a bullshitter, okay?"

Rick made for the open doors. "I'm getting a coffee. Anyone else?"

Melanie shook her head but Geoff said he'd have one.

When Rick had disappeared, Melanie asked Geoff what he thought had happened to everyone.

"I have absolutely no idea. No idea at all. None of it makes any sense." He plopped onto the rail beside her and leaned forward on his knees. "We drove down to Dawson... same thing: everywhere silent and deserted. Abandoned cars smashed through store windows, truck upturned in the street. Jeez, Mel, I'm worried."

She threw the butt to the ground and put her hand on his hands. "Don't be. We're okay, that's the main thing."

"But what if they've all gone for good? What if we're... what if we're the last people on the planet?"

"We won't be."

"Why not? And anyways, we don't even know why *we* weren't taken or—" he waved a hand in the air "—disintegrated...or whatever it was that happened."

The sound of footsteps made them both turn.

"Maybe we just live right," Johnny said. He was leaning against the door drinking Coca-Cola from a can, wrap-around dark glasses reflecting the sun. He looked like a young Marlon Brando: scuffed motorcycle boots, tight jeans and tight sweatshirt with the short sleeves rolled up onto his shoulders...a bulge of a cigarette pack in the left one, like a rectangular epaulette. He exuded attitude.

"Doesn't make any sense," Geoff said again.

Melanie got to her feet and threw coffee grounds onto the soil at the side of the path. "Have you noticed how there are no birds?" She walked a little way to the Dodge, its engine clicking in the heat. "And no insects?"

"There ain't no nothing," Johnny announced. "Took everything, whatever it was."

"But why not us?"

"That, Geoffrey, is the $64,000 question."

Melanie threw her head back and sniffed. "You think maybe it's poisonous...the air, I mean?"

Johnny shook his head. "Whatever happened happened fast — if it was something in the air then we'd have noticed it long before now." He stepped out and shucked himself onto the rail. "It was the light. I didn't see it — as you know — but that's what it was."

"Maybe it was a comet or something."

Melanie looked across at her husband. "Like that movie...*Day Of The Triffids*? That was some kind of comet, wasn't it?" She glanced over at the grassland rolling down the side of the valley to make sure she couldn't see any monster plants staggering up to keep them company.

"But whatever it was," Johnny said, his voice soft but insistent, "it still doesn't explain why it didn't do us. And it doesn't explain what's happened to all the bodies."

Melanie shook her head and went inside.

"We were inside," Geoff suggested. "But, no, that doesn't work either. Lots of folks — in fact, pretty much everyone — were inside, most of them in bed. Like you," he added.

Johnny looked back to make sure Melanie hadn't reappeared. "But not New York," he said. "New York is three hours in front of us."

Geoff let out a deep sigh. "Then it's happened all over the world."

Johnny took a slug of soda and nodded. "Could be."

"Except for us."

"Except for us." Johnny took another slug of soda and crushed the can.

"So it wasn't simply being inside that helped us," Geoff said, studying his tented fingers. "And it wasn't anything to do with here—" he waved a hand at the surrounding hillside "—because all the birds are gone."

"And the insects," Johnny added with a chuckle.

"Yeah, every cloud has its silver lining."

They both laughed.

Geoff got to his feet and looked at the station building. "So maybe it's got something to do with our building that doesn't apply to any others."

"Either that or we've been spared."

Geoff looked across at Johnny to see if he was smiling. "You serious?"

Johnny shrugged and pulled his pack of cigarettes from his sleeve. "Why not? Makes as much sense as anything else."

"Well I don't feel like Bruce Willis right now. Or Schwarzenegger. Truth told, I feel more like Woody Allen." He turned back to face the station. "Nope, it's the station. Has to be."

"Okay: why? Why the station?"

Geoff clapped his hands together in frustration. "God, I just don't know — the roof? Something in the concrete, maybe?"

"Like what?"

"Johnny—"

"I'm not being difficult — at least not deliberately — I'm just trying to eliminate the things that don't make any sense."

"*None* of it makes any sense."

"Agreed. But special concrete makes less sense than most things."

"Yeah, okay. So not the concrete."

"What about us? I mean, us ourselves?"

Geoff shook his head. "If it were just me and Rick then maybe that would work...our being brothers. But you and Mel, too...it doesn't work."

"Hey, what about something to do with the station itself?"

"I don't follow you."

Johnny blew smoke up into the air as he jumped from the rail. "The station...broadcasting!"

Geoff's eyes narrowed as he considered it.

"Sound wa— no, not sound waves...radio waves," Johnny continued. "Maybe there's something about radio waves that protected us. I mean, we pump a lot out from here, right?"

Geoff waggled his head from side to side, not really having an answer. This is the time, he thought, we suddenly need for one of us to have majored in some-damned-thing-or-other...to suddenly spout up with an answer for everything, just like they used to do in the comic books and those cheesy old black-and-white movies they kept showing on the SciFi channel, the ones starring Richard Carlson or Marshall Thompson.

He looked across at Johnny, the thirty-something dyslexic Lothario with the Springsteen wardrobe and the in-your-face deejay patter. Then he thought of his kid brother, twenty-eight-going-on-fifty, still unable to drive a car almost half a year after an accident that just wasn't his fault...and Melanie, beautiful Melanie, a siren in military-style baggy dungarees whose body sang him to sleep most nights when it was she — the high school drop-out with the background of parental abuse — who most needed the attention.

And himself, The Proprietor of KMRT — K-Mart, as the guys in town delighted in calling it — the failed advertising executive who couldn't stand the rat race, staring the big four-oh down the throat and not liking the smell that came out of there...a smell like flowers that had passed their prime, old perfume gone still and bad. Atomic Knights they were not. If the future of the planet — of mankind itself, maybe — were their responsibility then maybe it was time to send the audience home. The game was as good as finished even before it had gotten started.

"Hello...Planet Earth to Geoff...come in, Geoff..."

He shook his head and gave a weak smile. "Sorry. Drifting."

"Uh huh. Drifting where, oh great one?"

He reached over and lifted Johnny's pack of Marlboro from the concrete standing by his feet. "Just drifting." He shook a cigarette out and Johnny tossed across a matchbook, most of whose matches were twisted out and bent over, their heads blackened like dead soldiers. He pulled a match free, struck it, held it to the cigarette and inhaled. It tasted good... tasted normal.

He looked up at the sky through the blue-gray of the swirling smoke and said, "There's one thing we haven't said anything about."

"Yeah?"

"What happens tonight? What happens if they — or it... whatever it was — what happens if it comes back to finish the job?"

Johnny looked around again. Geoff thought it must be because of Melanie: Johnny didn't want to say anything that might cause her concern. Geoff liked that. It raised Johnny in his esteem and he made a mental note to have a word with Rick to get off his case...not ride him so much. They all needed each other's support if they were going to get through this, whatever 'this' was.

"...already given that some thought," Johnny was saying. "Right at the start, when Mel and me figured out for ourselves that the world had suddenly gone AWOL and we were left holding the hill against the enemy...I wondered if

— if this thing has been an intentional thing by—" he waved his hands in the air "—by whatever, then maybe they know we're here. Maybe they know they screwed up with the people up on the hill in that wacky-looking building with all the antennae sticking out of the top." He frowned and lowered his voice. "And maybe they're going to come back for us...tonight."

"So you're suggesting?"

"We get the hell out. Now!" He slapped the rail with his hand and the ring on his finger made a dull chime.

"That's fine if—" He tapped his index finger. "—One, 'they' know they screwed up and, two, 'they' know where they can get us. But it's a bad idea if they just send the light again, same way they did this morning, and we're suddenly out there, somewhere, away from whatever it was that protected us."

Johnny was nodding. "Hadn't thought it through that way. Maybe they won't come back: maybe it was just a random thing...something that happens once in every zillion years or so...something natural." He said the word 'natural' as though it was something unpleasant.

"Maybe."

"But you don't think so."

"No, I don't think so. I never heard of anything natural that could remove folks from out of their beds and out of their cars, just like that." He snapped his fingers. "Except maybe in *The X Files*."

"So they're coming back."

Geoff nodded, took a final pull on the butt and flicked it onto the path.

"So, which one is it to be? Move off or stay put here?"

Geoff leaned back and breathed out a final cloud of smoke. "You're putting *me* in charge?" he asked, tapping himself in the chest incredulously.

"Seems to me like you're the best we've got."

"Well, that convinces me what a sorry state we're in."

"And it's Amen to that, oh Great One."

They both forced a smile at that and turned to watch the sun, lost in their own thoughts as, silently and slowly, it made its way across to the far horizon. They couldn't see it doing it, of course. But they knew that it was.

Seven

It was almost eight p.m., the sun so low in the western sky that only the burnt orange memory of it remained over the wooded hills surrounding distant Carlisle, when Geoff and Rick were finally satisfied they had secured the station for the night.

In the hours since Geoff's conversation with Johnny, the four of them had been busy. Geoff had assumed the mantle of Chief of Operations, a role that had seemed to meet with everyone's approval. He had sent Johnny and Rick back into Jesman's Bend to get provisions while he and Melanie went around the station shoring up shutters and doorways and windows. Then they cleared the garage space of all the junk they had collected over the months, making room for the Dodge.

They watched in silence, each of them lost in their own thoughts, as the overhead door closed on its electronic pulley...stuttering the way it always did around the half-way mark, when Geoff had to slap the remote with his hand before pressing the button again. It caught with the one slap — it usually took more when they were raising the door, which is why they had abandoned the garage as a store for the Dodge in the first place — but when it *did* start again, there seemed an element of finality to it...and Geoff looked down at the remote with the steady confidence that he would never use it again...as though he would never open that door again. He looked across at Melanie and forced a smile when he saw her watching him, frowning. He waved the remote. "I love these things, you know."

"So I see. What is it they say about little things pleasing little minds?"

He leaned over, kissed the side of her face and gave her a knowing wink. "There's a couple bigger things I get a lot of fun out of, too." He brushed his hand lightly against Melanie's breasts and gave a lascivious grin.

Melanie shook her head in mock disgust and pushed him away. "God, you are such a sleazebag, you know that?"

Geoff smiled as the descending door removed the last glimmer of the Dodge and the door clanked to a stop. "There, that should do it," he said.

He turned to Melanie to hand her the remote for a second but she was pulling weeds from the side of the concrete apron. Geoff hadn't the heart to disturb her, lost as she was in the simple act of tending and tidying. He bent down and laid the remote on the ground and went across to check the door. It was secure. It rattled in its runners, but it was secure. Geoff reckoned that anyone with the capability of doing what they'd done would probably be able to beat down a few doors but he had kept that to himself. The chances were, anyway, that everyone else recognized that same fact but they, too, had kept it quiet. The activity had kept them all busy.

"All done?" Melanie asked.

Geoff turned and nodded, smiling at the tufts of weed in his wife's clenched hand. "How about you?"

Melanie frowned and then saw Geoff looking at her hand. She let out a high-pitched giggle and tossed the weeds across at him, Geoff ducking and dodging back around her to the door. Melanie chased him and, when the station door was satisfactorily locked and bolted, she fell into his arms.

In that embrace they were lost and they were safe, a million miles away from the strangeness of the deserted town and the abandoned trucks and cars, a thousand light years away from marauding lights in the night sky.

"I love you, honey," Geoff said, his voice little more than a whisper.

Melanie nodded, blinking her eyes once. A wave of profound sadness washed over her and, just for a second, she felt that they would never leave this place...and that this was the final embrace she would share with her husband.

"Hey," Geoff said, tapping Melanie's nose with his finger. "Lose those bad thoughts."

"How'd you know—"

"It's my job," he said.

Melanie rose onto the tips of her toes and found Geoff's mouth with her own, flicking her tongue across into his tongue, closing her eyes in the throes of the immense and indescribable pleasure of their touching, and of his smell.

Johnny and Rick had returned a little before five, quiet and even solemn. Geoff hadn't asked them about town — there was no reason to do so: he'd seen it for himself. Instead, while Melanie set to work making fresh coffee and plates of sandwiches, Geoff had watched the two men unloading bags of canned goods and bread into the station's large galley kitchen, filling cupboards and stacking things until the assembled produce coupled with the seemingly impervious security had made them all feel a little easier. Even *Gung ho.*

As the afternoon had trembled over into early evening — and the shadows lengthened and lengthened until, the light going fast, they faded into watery gray stains and then disappeared completely — Geoff had Rick and Johnny take half-hour turns sitting on the roof with Geoff's old binoculars, keeping a watch for any sign of movement on the road leading down into town.

With the lessening light had come the lowering temperature and, a little after 7:30, Geoff watched Rick finish securing the shutters on most of the windows. It was the final job that needed to be done. Geoff had said that it was probably best that they kept lighting to a minimum, and even then only as absolutely necessary. Rick stepped back, lost for a moment in the results of his work, and then suddenly remembered that when they went in they would be in the dark. He turned and gave a half-hearted smile.

"Done?"

Rick nodded and looked around. It had all the appearances of a final look, a last glance before they slipped the black bag over his head and then the noose. "I used to love this time of the evening at this time of year," Rick said.

There was a softness to the words and to Rick's voice that Geoff hadn't heard before. Or, at least, he didn't recall hearing them. Rick sighed. "But now, with all the noises gone, and us—" He waved a hand at the gathering gloom and nodded to the station. "—scurrying around in there in total darkness like moles, it's like..." He searched for the words. "It's like I'm standing in a painting...or in one of those hologram set-ups on the Star Trek shows. Like the dinosaurs in the *Jurassic Park* movies — everything seems to be there but when you get up close to it, it's not the same." He looked around at his brother and made a face. "Am I making any sense here or just blowing wind?"

"Yes, you're making a lot of sense."

The countryside seemed to be sitting out there, waiting...but waiting for what? That was the question. There was no sound, no light and no energy anywhere in the world. Geoff imagined flying up into space, right from where he was standing, and soaring over the towns and the cities, over the plains and the forests, over the multi-lane highways and the towering skyscrapers...all of them empty, silent and deserted.

"You coming in?" Johnny's voice broke the stillness.

"Yeah, we're all done out here. See anything?"

"Uh uh. Quiet as the grave."

Geoff would have preferred a different analogy but he took the point.

"Isn't this about the place in the story where you're supposed to say 'It's quiet...*too* quiet!'?"

"Yeah," Rick said, ever the movie buff, "like the old Foreign Legion movies or the Indian uprisings, where a handful of guys are stuck in the fort with a bunch of their dead comrades propped up on the battlements, hoping to fend off one final attack before the cavalry arrive."

"Think they'll get here, Geoff?" Johnny shouted down from the roof. "The cavalry, I mean."

Geoff didn't think so. He didn't think there was anyone to help them repel this enemy, whatever it was and wherever it had come from. But he wasn't about to tell them that. The secret of good leadership is to preserve optimism, even in the face of insurmountable odds. But "it'll turn out," was as much as he could manage, and even that stuck in his throat like a fishbone.

"Yeah," Johnny said, and he moved back on the roof and sat down against the door. Out of sight of Geoff and Rick.

"You really think that? That it'll be okay?"

With a final look around outside, his hands thrust deep into the pockets of his denims, Geoff silently bid the world goodnight. Then he said, "Yes, I really think that."

He turned around and stepped into the station.

Rick followed him and Geoff locked the door, dropping the two security deadbolts into place. The sound was like a cell door and the darkness that engulfed them was like a waiting grave.

All that was then left to do was check the windows and join the others.

"I was wondering," Rick said as they made their way up to the studio, having satisfied themselves that the building was as secure as they were likely to be able to make it. He was carrying a small pencil flashlight that cast a shuddering circle of white on the floor in front of them.

Geoff said, "What about?"

"How long will the food last? I mean, you know...if everyone *has* gone and we're the last people—" He stopped himself saying 'alive' and just left it at that.

Geoff held open the door to the main corridor. "We *won't* be the last people. Something will—"

"But if we are, how long will the food last?"

Geoff led the way to the studio, trailing a hand along the wall for guidance. "Indefinitely. The canned stuff, years certainly."

At the door to the sound booth, Rick stopped and pulled on his brother's arm. "And if there are no animals? Nothing to kill and eat?"

Geoff punched him lightly in the shoulder. "Then we'll become vegetarian. Learn to grow things. Vegetables." He opened the door and Melanie looked up from the console. Johnny was in the studio shielded by the soundproof glass, bent over a box of CDs with a candle glimmering beside him and the pinpoint glow of the system lights above his head.

"All secure, Number One?" she asked, shielding her eyes from the flashlight's beam.

Geoff saluted. "Aye aye, Captain."

Johnny stood up and waved a CD case, suddenly surprised to see Geoff and Rick in the sound booth with Melanie. He leaned over the desk and dislodged a stack of CD cases, then flicked the mic on the desk. "Shit, can't see a damned thing in here," he announced. "Anyway, I found it." He glanced an apology to Geoff. "I was getting lonely out there — and it's so quiet. I thought we could liven things up with a little music." He sniggered.

Melanie smiled. "Found what?"

Johnny waved for her to wait and fumbled the CD into the console deck, turning the control dial. He pressed a button and then stood back, the broad grin on his face illuminated by the candle's glow.

The strains of The Carpenters' 'Calling Occupants Of Interplanetary Craft' filled the booth. Melanie laughed up at Geoff and Rick. She laughed even louder, clapping her hands, when Geoff pointed for her to look in the studio: Johnny was standing, legs and arms outstretched — the candle in his right hand — swaying side to side to the music.

Rick thrust his hands into his pants pockets. "So what do we do now?"

"Now," Geoff said, "we wait."

It was just past nine o'clock.

Eight

In the hours that followed, once they had satisfied themselves that the station was reasonably secure, the quartet ate a light supper of cold meats and salad, cheese-topped breadcakes filled with pate and humus, coleslaw and pickles, and then, while Johnny had played his hard rock session leading to midnight, Melanie, Geoff and Rick sat out on the roof staring across the quiet and empty world. When the night finally spilled into one o'clock and it was Melanie's turn at the turntable — they still called it 'the turntable' even though most of the music was now played from a three-disc CD set-up — Rick and Geoff agreed to have a last smoke before turning in.

There was something inexplicably threatening about the silent blackness of the trees across the valley that made the pair uncomfortable and, without saying anything about their thoughts to each other, they sat in silence yearning for the sanctity of the station. Feeble though they were in the grand terms of the cosmos and whatever things might be marauding their way through it, the walls of the station seemed to promise some kind of barrier to all that might be out there. Maybe, Geoff thought as he took a last lingering look at the outside world, that was how the people had felt back in the 1950s when they carried out those ridiculous safety precautions against atomic bomb attacks — hiding under flimsy wooden tables with their hands over their ears — or like squirrels and rabbits that curled themselves up against the wheels of an oncoming car.

They went inside without speaking.

It was almost two o'clock when the light came again.

Johnny and Geoff were asleep — Johnny in his room and Geoff on a cushioned camping mat stretched out on the floor in the sound booth — and Rick was sitting across from Geoff reading *Mad* magazine in the glow of the flashlight, with his feet propped on the CD shelves. Melanie was playing tunes and songs and huskily breathing her patter into the mic, hoping against all reason that someone would call her on the telephone...if for no other reason than to complain. It was an interesting playlist after all, the usual late night/early morning aural fodder of Bennett, Sinatra, Holliday and Mitchell having given way to The Chemical Brothers, Philip Glass, Will Smith and Captain Beefheart. As the strains of Frank and the Mothers' 'Bobby Brown' faded, the world went white.

Rick jumped to his feet dropping his magazine.

"Wh-What's up?" Geoff rolled to one side and thumped his head on the table leg. "Shit!" he said, rubbing the side of his head as he squinted up at his brother. "That hurt. You say something?" he asked groggily.

"The light. It came again." Rick was at the glass looking into the candlelit studio. Melanie was looking around her, checking to see if anything had changed.

"Go get Johnny," Geoff said. As Rick left the booth, Geoff leaned over and switched on the connecting mic. "You okay, Mel?"

Melanie nodded. And then, as though reconsidering her first answer, she gave a shrug. Who the hell knew? It was a fair point.

"Now what?"

Geoff allowed the question to sink in while craning his head to one side to see if he could pick up any sounds from outside. *Now what?*

He looked around the booth, searching for an answer. Then his gaze settled on the telephone sitting on the table.

When he looked up again, Melanie was pulling the broadcasting mic towards her. Geoff hammered on the window and shook his head. "Not yet," he said. "Let's just wait a while, find out if anything's happened."

"Why don't I make an announcement? See if anyone's there."

Geoff shook his head again and lit a candle — Rick had taken the flashlight with him to get Johnny. "No, not yet."

"Can I at least put a record on?"

Geoff thought on that one a minute. What was the harm in that? *Well,* a small voice said lazily, in a small back room inside Geoff's head, *the harm in that is letting folks know we're still here — isn't that why you're wandering around in the darkness?* "No," he said, trying to sound casual...like there was some damned good reason — maybe there was a damned good reason but Geoff couldn't actually visualize it. "Let's not do anything yet."

Melanie sat back down and lit a cigarette. "I'm smoking too much," she said, her voice thick with disappointment in herself. "But the light is just so good."

When Rick came into the booth with Johnny in tow, the flashlight beam playing around their feet, Geoff had the telephone handset in one hand and was keying in numbers with the other.

"Anything?" Johnny asked around a yawn.

Rick switched off the flashlight and said, "Who you calling?"

"Sheriff's office."

Geoff finished keying and waited. The phone rang.

"We gonna go outside?" Johnny said. "See if anything's happening."

Geoff glanced into the studio and watched his wife — or, more accurately, Mel's cigarette tip — swinging side to side in the swivel chair, in small erratic movements.

Rick said, "Shit, nobody's there."

"Come on, let's do it," Johnny said. "Let's go outside."

Geoff was about to hang up but Melanie stopped him. "Give them a couple of minutes."

Geoff hit the squawk button and dropped the receiver onto the cradle. The sound of the telephone *brrrrt-brrrrt*ing all the way down in Jesman's Bend sounded sad and lonely. Around the *brrrrt*s, Rick said, "Anything's better than just sitting here." He turned around with his back to both Johnny and Geoff and then turned back. He ran his hands through his hair and took a deep sigh. "I mean, that's what we were waiting for...isn't it? We were waiting for the light...and we got it. So let's go out and—"

Geoff raised his hand.

Rick frowned petulantly.

Johnny said, "What?"

Geoff turned to looked down at the phone. It was silent.

"It stopped ringing," Johnny said.

"Hey, you win tonight's star pri—"

"Quiet, Rick." Geoff watched the phone, leaned closer to the squawkbox.

"Whyn't you pick it up, for crissakes?"

Geoff looked at his brother. Then at the telephone. No, it *wasn't* silent — there was a sound coming from it, but what was it?

"You know," Johnny said, his voice soft and careful, "you know what that sounds like?"

Geoff looked at him.

"It sounds like someone listening."

Geoff returned his attention to the telephone. That was what he had heard. Johnny was absolutely right — maybe it was something inherent in human beings...that you actually could hear when someone was listening to you on the phone. He'd done it plenty of times, called someone up and asked them something and then he had actually been able to hear them thinking...or, indeed, listening. It wasn't a sound of breathing or of movement, but simply of existing.

Hey mom, someone's existing *on the phone.*

Yeah, well make sure they clean it up when they're through.

Mel's voice broke the silence. "What's happening out there?"

Geoff hit the audio button killing the dead sound and then hit it again. The dial tone sounded friendly and reassuring. He re-dialed quickly.

"Geoff?" Mel said. Her voice sounded scared.

"It's okay," he said.

No it isn't, the voice in Geoff's head whispered. *It isn't okay at all and you know it.*

No sooner had the final number connected then the busy tone echoed around the booth. It sounded for all the world like an early warning siren.

Geoff hit the audio button and the tone stopped. He stepped back from the table.

Johnny plucked a cigarette from the Marlboro pack with his mouth. "Maybe someone picked it up and—" He lit up and continued around a cloud of smoke. "—and they didn't want to say anything."

Rick moved over to the chair and plopped into it. "Know what I think?" he said, "What about if maybe—" He used his hands to suggest a surface and objects above that surface. "—maybe the vibrations of the telephone's ringing unsettled something and—"

"Aw, come on, man!"

"Shut the fuck up, Johnny and let me finish, okay?" Rick turned back to his brother. "So, the vibrations of the phone unsettle something, like something on a shelf above the desk...a manual or something. Anyway, and this something drops down onto the desk and—" He clapped his hands together. "Blam! Knocks the receiver off the hook."

Johnny blew smoke and shook his head.

"Hey, all I'm saying is it could happen, right?" He ignored Johnny and looked at Geoff. "*Right?*"

Melanie came through the linking door to the studio. "Mind if I join in?"

Nobody answered.

"Geoff, all I'm saying is it *could* happen, right?"

"Okay, it could happen." He hit the audio button and re-dialed again.

"Who you calling, honey?"

Geoff held a finger to his lips.

The final number clicked home and for a second nothing happened. Then the familiar noise of a ringing tone sounded. Geoff hit the audio key and clasped his hands around his stomach.

"Oh God," Rick said, his voice sounding small in the cramped booth.

"Will someone tell me what's going on?"

Johnny put his arm around Melanie's shoulder. "What's going on, dear Melvin, is another book has just bounced off of Don Patterson's desk and flipped his phone receiver back onto the cradle." He shook his head. "I mean, shit like that could make Ripley's 'Believe It Or Not'."

"We have to go out," Geoff said. "We have to go outside and take a look around."

Johnny dropped his butt to the floor and ground it with his boot heel. "Now why did I just *know* you were going to say that."

Nine

The night was cool and the sky was clear. It was 2:37, and it was refreshingly lighter and less claustrophobic than the darkened station.

Geoff went out onto the roof first, turning off the flashlight beam while they were in the corridor and even then squeezing through the outer door so as to avoid any suggestion of movement should anyone be watching the side of the station. He wasn't taking any chances. When Rick asked why, Geoff simply shrugged. Melanie followed with Rick.

Keeping his back to the outside wall, Rick edged his way to where the small wall started and then crouched down. On all fours, he scurried crab-like along the wall's side until he was in the center, overlooking the valley and the beginning of the forest road. There, immediately beneath the station, the road crept to the right as though it was going straight down the side of Honeydew Mountain and then hit a fork: the right hand tine of the fork carried on towards I-90 while the left snaked around to travel the full length of the exposed saddle and ran down into the woods that led on into Jesman's Bend.

Once he was in place, Rick shifted into a sitting position and lifted his head so that he could see over the wall.

It was Melanie who broke the silence. "See anything?"

Without turning around, Rick shook his head. "Don't know what I'm looking for," he said. "But there's nothing unusual."

The outer door squeaked open behind them and Johnny emerged onto the roof. He held out a pair of binoculars to Geoff. "Try these," he said. "They've got infra red."

Geoff took them and duck-waddled across to his brother.

"Why'd you buy those?" Melanie asked in a trembling voice. She was feeling a chill in her bones that had nothing to do with the temperature and everything to do with the clandestine nature of being on the roof, speaking in whispers with the lights out.

"Dunno," Johnny said. "Seemed like a good idea at the time, I guess."

Melanie nodded, apparently satisfied with the answer, and watched Rick lift the glasses to his eyes.

Johnny suddenly craned his head back. "Hey, you hear that?"

Geoff hissed for him to keep quiet.

"What?" Melanie whispered.

"Listen."

They listened.

"I don't hear anything except the crickets," Melanie said at last, unable to keep the trace of exasperation out of her voice.

"Kee rect," Johnny said. "The crickets. They're back."

"Oh ye—"

"What's that?" Geoff whispered loudly, pointing across the valley where, just for a second or two, a light had shone out of the blackness.

Rick moved the glasses over to the left of where he had been looking. "Where?" he said. "What was it?"

Geoff shifted to the other side of his brother and rested his chin on the wall. "I don't know...but it was something. A light of some kind."

"Like a flashlight?"

"Let me have the glasses." Rick handed them over and hunkered down. "It was around about—" Keeping his elbows on the wall so as to steady himself, and keeping his head, neck and hands in perfect unison, Geoff slowly moved his sweep of vision along the forest road to where the trees grew dense. "—round about where we saw Jerry Borgesson's truck."

"So what kind of light was it?"

"Does it matter?" Geoff said.

"What I mean is," Rick said, lowering his voice so that Melanie and Johnny couldn't hear him, "could it have been the cab's interior light?"

Geoff didn't answer right away. Then he said, "Yes, it could have been that." He lowered the glasses. "How'd you fancy a hike?"

"What, down the forest road to the truck?"

"It's the only thing I can think of." Geoff looked around and saw that Melanie and Johnny had moved across to the far side of the roof, overlooking the valley edge, away from the road. He turned back to his brother and said, "I just want us to be sure about what's happening before we let everyone know we're still here." He shrugged. "I know...maybe I'm being paranoid, but that thing with the phone. I mean, how come nobody said anything? You know as well as I do that someone had picked the receiver up...but they didn't speak." He watched his wife leaning over the roof, saw Johnny hold onto her waist and lean over alongside her. "Then they put the receiver back. There was somebody there...I know there was. But they didn't speak. Or—" He stopped and looked down at the binoculars cradled in his lap. "Or maybe they couldn't speak."

"How do you mean? Like they were being held captive or something?"

"Or something."

Rick let out a low whistle that was more air than note.

"And now, maybe Jerry *is* back at his truck. Right now. Maybe he's down there, crawling about on the floor of his cab trying to figure out what's wrong with it. And then again, maybe it's not Jerry."

"Hey, maybe there's nobody there at all."

Geoff nodded, tapping the binocular side with the ring on his middle finger. "Yeah, that too. But the way I figure it is we don't want to start driving around drawing attention to ourselves until we know what's going on...or until we've at least got a reasonable idea and we've verified that things are almost back to the way they were before the first light hit."

"Okay. We walk down to Jerry's truck and see what's happening."

Geoff slapped Rick's knee and made to get up.

"But Geoff," Rick said. "What if...what if, you know, things aren't the way they were...or the way they should be? What then?"

The faint and far-off sound of an engine turning over prevented Geoff from having to respond. Melanie and Johnny ran across, each of them whooping with joy at the sudden return to familiarity, but Geoff snapped for them to keep quiet and get down out of sight.

"Hey, what's the matter, man?" Johnny whined. He pulled himself against the wall next to Geoff while Melanie, frowning, put her arm around her husband's shoulder. "Jerry's trying to get his truck started." He shrugged. "So what's the big deal?"

"Yeah, we can go down into town and find out what happened to everybody," Rick added.

Geoff was still looking through the binoculars when the engine fired into life. When he spoke it was a mutter. "You know, I'd've bet a dollar to a dime he'd never get that thing started."

"So what's so bad about that?" Johnny asked, peering over the wall as he watched the distant road leading down into Jesman's Bend. The sound of the truck driving off was now unmistakable.

"And there's something else."

"What?"

Geoff handed the glasses over to Johnny. "Here, take a look."

Johnny raised the glasses and scanned the road until he caught sight of the old truck moving down the road, disappearing for a few seconds each time a clump of trees came between it and the station. Johnny grunted.

"What is it?" Melanie said.

"Hey." Rick's voice was little more than a throaty whisper. "He doesn't have his lights on."

"Well, first off he gets the truck started," Geoff said quietly to Melanie, "which is pretty good going considering the thing was on fire when we last saw it. And then he drives without his lights on."

Johnny tutted. "So? Maybe they were damaged in the crash." He handed the glasses back to Geoff.

Geoff nodded. "Yeah, maybe so. I guess it's surprising that there's any life left at all in the engine. But if there is life there, then I'd've thought there'd be enough for the lights. But there's another thing."

Johnny sighed. "What?"

"How fast do you reckon he's going?" He cut across Johnny's and Rick's groans. "I mean, approximately."

Rick's face grimaced. "Thirty, thirty-five?"

Geoff nodded. "At least. And we all know what that road's like, yeah? It bends and turns and winds like piece of dropped string."

"What are you saying, honey?"

"What I'm saying is that Jerry's driving that truck like a stock car racer." He looked through the glasses again and then put them down, turning around and slumping with his back against the wall. "He's out of sight now, heading into the last stretch before town."

They all slumped back alongside Geoff, like condemned men facing a firing squad. Melanie was the first one to break the silence.

"Maybe it doesn't mean anything, Geoff. Could be a lot of reasons."

The truth, however, was that she couldn't think of one. Geoff was right: the road down through the trees into Jesman's Bend was treacherous and, even if his lights were *not* working and he was still determined to get into town, Jerry Borgesson would have driven a lot slower. Over the years, many experienced locals had fallen foul of misjudging the tight bends on the Forest Road...and that was often in daylight or with their lights on. Jerry driving the truck away at a fast speed in total darkness didn't make a lot of sense at all. And they all knew it...deep down, where it really mattered.

"So what do we do now?"

Geoff turned to his brother. "Well, we decide — democratically. My view is that two of us walk down into town, while it's dark. That way, maybe we can find out some more." He shrugged and tried a big smile. "Hey, it could be that there's nothing, right? Could be that Jerry was just busting to get into town and his lights weren't working and he thought, *fuck it: I'm going anyways...and I'm going as fast as I can.* We don't know what these folks have been through...or even where they've been through it, so we maybe have to make a few allowances for strange behavior."

"But we should still be cautious...is that what you're saying?"

Geoff nodded and slapped Rick's leg. "We should still be cautious."

"So, who's it gonna be?" Johnny asked, verbalizing everyone's thoughts. "Who's the lucky twosome?"

Ten

Maybe it wasn't entirely democratic but, to Geoff, the way they had decided on who was going to go out into the night made a lot of sense.

Geoff was first up because...well, because he was effectively in charge. It wasn't put quite so bluntly during their brief discussion but it was understood that Geoff seemed to have the best handle on what was going on, so it seemed logical that he was out there making decisions as events presented themselves.

Melanie stayed behind because she was the expert when it came to transmitting, and if Geoff and whoever didn't return from their expedition, then transmitting needed to be a real weapon in their limited arsenal. Geoff had no idea why he should not return but there were so many unanswered things that he was playing it safe.

Playing it safe also mean that Melanie — who figured large in all of Geoff's considerations — was reasonably mobile. And the problem there was that Melanie didn't drive. She had taken a few lessons with her father, back when she was sixteen, but she had never pursued driving as such, being content, as were most New Yorkers, to take the subway, buses or, on special occasions, cabs when she needed to go somewhere. This meant that Geoff had to leave a driver behind, which excluded his brother from the list of possibles. Ever since the accident, more than six months ago now, Rick had been unable even to consider driving. When he simply got behind a steering wheel, Rick would break out in cold sweats...shaking hands, dried-up mouth, the full business. So leaving his brother to look after his wife wasn't an option for Geoff.

And so it was decided.

Geoff and Rick stepped out from one darkness and into another at 3:11.

With a soft smile and a final stroke on her husband's arm, Melanie stepped back into the station and allowed Johnny to secure the door. Rick watched, wondering whether to say anything but, glancing around at the road which disappeared into the night, he didn't feel very reassuring.

Away from the pull-in apron in front of the station doors, the road drifted gently downhill. They kept to the grass sides to avoid even the slightest noise of their shoes on the blacktop, coat collars pulled up against the night. It felt strange to be out there at this time, but the sound of an occasional rustle and cricket *chirrup*s from the undergrowth made for company of sorts. It also made for several jumps as each of them thought that the sounds meant that someone was sneaking up on them. But that didn't make sense, any more than their being out here in the first place made sense, and pretty soon they had moved into muted conversation.

As they turned left to head on down to town, Geoff stopped and looked back at the station, nestled into the side of Honeydew Mountain. He would have given anything to be up there right now, just passing time, doing this and that, chatting to his brother and maybe Johnny, listening to Mel's show. He gave a single wave to the station and turned to face the road, suddenly aware that Rick was watching him.

"You okay?"

"I'm fine."

Rick pushed his hands still further into his jacket pockets, at the same time hugging it tight around his legs. "How far to town?"

"From here? Three miles maybe. Four at the outside." Geoff kicked a stone and sent it spinning into the long grass. "Should be there in an hour, hour and a quarter if we take it slow and easy."

"Well..." Rick stepped out and began to walk, bending his head back, taking in the stars and the endless blackness of space. "Let's just hope we get a lift back."

Geoff said, "And it's a big Amen to that."

"At least this way it's downhill."

Geoff grunted acknowledgment. No matter how hard he tried and no matter how optimistic he allowed himself to become, he could not imagine that they would be getting a lift back to the station. In fact, he already felt that he would never see his wife again. Right now, walking down the road, that realization was easier than it had been back at the station. Back at the station, with Melanie framed in the doorway, there were options open to him: for one thing, he could change his mind and stay put. But now, with the wind on his face and in his hair, and his coat around him, he felt primed for action. A *grunt*, deep *In Country* and miles from home, prepared for whatever the enemy threw at him.

As they reached the spot where they had seen Jerry Borgesson's truck, Geoff realized that he had seen the same thoughts captured in Melanie's eyes. She too didn't expect him to be back. He took his hands out of his pockets and, with his right hand, felt for the gold band that had been there since their wedding day. It felt good. Whatever happened, nobody could take that away from him, or take away the years they had enjoyed together.

They stopped and looked around.

"See anything?" Geoff called to his brother.

Rick glanced back and when he saw that Geoff was watching him, he shook his head and continued to plod around the thick grass beside the road. After a couple of minutes they met again on the road and continued on towards Jesman's Bend.

They walked in silence for more than a half hour, Rick occasionally clearing his throat and glancing across at his brother, while Geoff merely forged ahead. He had worked his way into a routine, placing one foot after the other and mentally striking off the yards to town. And all the time he concentrated on sending a message to Melanie that told her how much he loved her and how she should not be bitter whatever happened to him tonight. Just now and then, he got a wave of guilt about dragging his brother along to share in whatever was waiting for them. But he hadn't had a choice. Maybe Rick would get around to driving again — and Geoff certainly hoped that was the case — but he could not leave it to chance, not when Mel's life was dependent on it. Then even that thought brought its own wave of guilt, as he realized he was effectively saying he didn't mind Johnny getting killed but he did mind if it was his brother. But surely everyone thought that way. What was it they said about blood being thicker than water?

Rick was aware of Geoff looking at him. He didn't respond. He was in what he called 'The graveyard', a place in his mind when he imagined a pair of dead people were walking along behind him...shuffling their tire-marked torsos and stretching out their wattled, sore-covered and blood-stained arms to reach for him. He knew the two of them well, though he had forgotten their names since the hearing. Sometimes he imagined they were right alongside him, standing back amidst the cover of the trees, ready to waddle out in that off-balance way the dead have of walking...and sometimes he imagined they were waiting up ahead, ready to step out into his path

hey, asshole, whyn't you come and finish the job...think there's a couple of bones here seem to be still in one piece

like a couple of old Wild West gunslingers. But mostly he thought they were behind him, moving one mud-caked foot after the other, gaining on him. He turned around and walked backwards a couple of steps while he scanned the road behind them. It was deserted.

"Hear something?" Geoff whispered.

Rick turned around and shook his head. "Just checking."

"Listen."

They stopped and listened.

Up ahead, occasionally hidden by the wind through the trees, was the unmistakable sound of industrious activity. A lot of activity.

Hammers hammered and engines *vroom-vroomed*, their sound muted and hoarse, straining. The wind picked up the sound like a playful dog, ran with it first one way and then the other, taking it out of earshot and then dropping it again, louder now.

"Sounds promising," Rick ventured. He glanced to his right at a big bush that seemed to be moving strangely, the way maybe a bush moves when a couple of dead people are holding it close to them. But it was just the wind, of course.

Geoff didn't say anything.

They walked a couple more steps and stopped again, both of them together. "Doesn't seem right to you either, does it?" Geoff said.

Rick had to admit that it didn't. It didn't sound right at all. The main thing that was wrong with it was that, even though the sound of activity was reasonably loud now, with the first houses just around the next clump of trees, there wasn't a single voice to be heard. No muted shouts or far-off conversation. No laughter, no music.

It's life, Geoff, but not as we know it.

Geoff hissed and pointed to the trees. Rick understood straight away. If they ducked off the road and into the trees before the bend, they could come up on the ridge that overlooked the town without anyone below being able to see them. That way they could check things out before actually having to advertise their presence.

Rick led the way through the bushes and checked behind every few steps to make sure that the lumbering sound of twigs and branches being either snapped or displaced was in fact his brother and not anyone else. The hoot of an owl from somewhere over to their right suddenly made Rick feel silly. What the hell were they doing clambering about in the woods when it was obvious that everything was entirely normal?

He pushed past a large branch, holding it to one side but failing to notice that the ground fell away into a deep ditch whose earthen sides were a maze of exposed roots. The sense of falling away was horrible. Rick felt as though he had stepped off the edge of the earth, and was doomed to plunge forever through space. He held onto the large branch with one hand and, even as his feet went away from him and he plunged forward, he threw up his free hand and grabbed the end of the branch, momentarily swinging forward and then being swept back into a huge bush. The branches cut and pierced his skin, one narrowly missing his eye and instead getting entangled in his hair. Rick let go of the branch and fell into the bush, settling after a few seconds and trying hard not to breathe loudly...though he suspected anyone within twenty yards would have heard all the commotion.

The hand on his arm made his jump but it was only Geoff, smiling despite his obvious concern at all the noise. "You okay?"

Rick allowed his brother to pull him to his feet and then rubbed himself down. He nodded. The branches had scratched his face and managed to tear open his jacket and shirt, and raise thick welts on his chest and stomach — he tucked his shirt back into his pants, wincing at the pain. "I'll live. Think anyone heard me?"

Geoff shrugged. "We'll wait a few minutes just to be on the safe side."

They waited and listened.

The noises of industrious work continued seemingly unabated and there were no tell-tale branch snaps or rustles to suggest that anyone had heard Rick's plight. Geoff patted Rick on the shoulder.

"Come on, I'll lead the way this time."

Geoff moved off. He slid slowly down into the ditch and waved for Rick to follow. As he moved away, Rick felt the unmistakable feeling that someone was watching him. At the top of the ditch, he turned around

hey, asshole, whyn't you...

but there was nobody there.

He slid down and followed Geoff across the floor of the ditch and then up the other side. They made their way slowly and with hardly any noise at all until they emerged once more at the side of the road. Ahead of them, they could see Main Street stretching over to the right and out of town towards Dawson.

There were no lights on, and hardly any moon, but what natural light there was enabled them to see that the folks down in Jesman's Bend were having problems sleeping. So they'd gathered in the town square where they had brought various vehicles onto the grass and were busy working on them.

"I don't get it," Rick whispered. "What the hell are they doing?"

"Never mind that," said Geoff, "why are they doing it without any lights?"

They watched and kept quiet. Then Rick said, "Geoff, they're all wearing dark glasses."

"And gloves," Geoff added.

Don Patterson stood up after being bent over into the engine of Luke Napier's Eldorado...which already seemed a little strange because Luke himself was across the street hitching some kind of wire siding to Martha McNeil's flatbed pick-up. "What—"

Geoff shook his head and put a finger up to his mouth.

After another couple of minutes of seemingly doing nothing, just standing there, Don glanced at a man alongside him and then slid behind the Eldorado's wheel. Rick couldn't tell for sure who the other man was but he limped out of Don's way like Jim Ferumern.

"You see that?" Rick whispered.

"What?"

"Yeah, it was Jim."

"No, you see the way he walked?"

Geoff nodded. One-time quarterback Jim Ferumern was walking like he'd shit himself, slow and easy straight-legged steps, his arms held awkwardly, each about a foot away from the side of his body.

Ferumern pulled the door closed and turned the ignition a couple of times until the engine caught. Then the others stepped back a few feet — each of them displaying the same cumbersome gait — while Luke Napier's Eldorado slowly lifted into the air, wobbled a couple of times and then dropped back to the ground. As Don got out of the car again, another vehicle — neither Rick nor Geoff could identify the make or figure out who the driver was — rose into the night sky from somewhere down Derwent Street and angled over

Main and moved slowly out to the east. Nobody on the town square so much as gave the vehicle a second look.

Neither Geoff nor Rick spoke.

They just watched.

Down towards the end of Main, a convertible pulled up into the sky out of the filling station. This one angled around and moved northwards.

Back down in the town square, Don Patterson was doing something beneath the Eldorado's hood. He stood up for a second and took off one of his gloves — then he bent over again.

Geoff slithered backwards and rested his head on the grass. "I think it's time we went back," he said.

Rick turned to face him, his eyes suddenly wide in either disbelief or outright fear. "Geoff—"

Geoff reached out a hand and steadied his brother. "Take it—"

"*Geoff!*" Rick hissed, nodding to something behind Geoff.

Geoff turned slowly and saw the imposing shape of Jerry Borgesson standing just a few yards to the side. Jerry was not looking at them. He was wearing dark glasses and he was standing straight-legged with his hands — his gloved hands — by his side staring down into the town square. All the activity from down below seemed to have stopped.

Geoff said, "Hey, Jerry..."

Jerry Borgesson turned slightly and half-looked in their direction, like a wily old fifth-grade teacher glancing at a couple of errant pupils he'd caught giving him the bird behind his back. They couldn't see Jerry's eyes through the dark glasses — real nifty-looking jobs, like the ones the fly-boys wore when they were flying billion-dollar stealth airplanes — but the expression on his face spoke eloquently. *Hoo, boy*, the expression seemed to say, *are you guys in for it* now!

Lifting his left leg outwards, causing him to sway a little, Jerry started to turn towards them. And then he lifted his arms and started pulling off his gloves.

Eleven

Melanie watched Geoff and Rick walk down the path away from the station with a sinking feeling in the pit of her stomach. She stepped back, half turning away while Johnny stepped forward and locked the door, pushing the dead bolt into place with a sound of grim finality.

"He'll be okay, Mel," Johnny said without turning around.

"I know," she said, though she wasn't exactly sure. "It's just that everything seems so...I dunno, so *strange*...I just don't feel comfortable with anything."

Turning around to face Melanie, with the sprawling radio station looming up and around her, empty, and without any shows being transmitted, Johnny knew exactly what she meant. Even the most familiar and dependable of things seemed to have assumed an air of mystery.

Melanie looked up at him and gave a trembling smile. He knew she was close to tears, fighting them back not just for her own sake but for his too.

"C'mon," he said, "let's go up on the roof. That way you can keep an eye on him, make sure he doesn't come to any harm." Even as he was saying it, Johnny wondered if he was doing the right thing. What if they were sitting up there watching Geoff being torn apart by some raging pissed-off flying-saucer-lagged lizard-monster from Alpha Centauri? *Yeah, but apart from that, Mrs. Grisham, how did you enjoy the show?*

But second thoughts were far too late. Melanie's eyes lit up like a kid's at Christmas, and Johnny didn't have the heart to sound a note of caution. It would teach him to think first before he spoke.

"That's a *great* idea." She ran ahead of Johnny and hit the stairs to the roof two at a time. "Quick, before they're out of sight."

"If you're gonna do it, Lizard-man, don't do it where we can see you," Johnny mumbled. Then he followed.

They crept out onto the roof, bent double, and made their way to the wall overlooking the concrete apron. The moon was about half-full and the clouds kept eating into what available light there was. Even so, they had a clear view of two figures making their way down the lane. As the figures reached the fork that turned left to head into town, one of them stopped and turned around. Johnny and Melanie couldn't make out who it was but Melanie knew deep in her heart that it was Geoff. "Take care, honey," she whispered to the night. Then, right on cue — as though he had acknowledged the communication — the figure waved his arm and turned around. And they continued down towards Jesman's Bend.

A few minutes later, they had disappeared behind the trees.

"What do you think they'll find?"

Johnny shrugged. "Well, either everyone is back or they're not." He patted his jacket pockets for his cigarettes.

Melanie slumped down against the wall and crossed her legs. "I hate it."

Johnny found the pack and shook a Marlboro free. "What? Him going off without you?"

She nodded. "Well, that. But it's the *waiting* that gets me." She drew her knees up and wrapped her arms around them. "It's the same when he's just going out to the store... even going out of the *room*. I don't like to be apart from him. You know what I mean?"

Johnny shrugged and lit the cigarette behind cupped hands. "I guess. I ain't never been that close to anybody. Not even my folks." He pulled on the Marlboro and blew out smoke. "I *was*," he added, "but then my pop died. Took a long time about it, too."

"What was it?"

"Cancer." He held up the cigarette. "Lungs. Only took him a couple of weeks to go once it had been diagnosed. But they were sad weeks. Seemed like forever."

"How old were you?"

"I dunno. Thirteen, maybe fourteen."

"You don't know exactly? Like what year he died?"

Johnny sat next to her and handed her the cigarette when she held out her hand. "Nope. He died. And that was that. Didn't seem important to know the year, or the day or the time."

"You must know the time!"

"It was late one night. I was watching TV and my mom called for me. I knew it was bad because her voice was strange."

"Strange how?"

He took the cigarette back and tapped the burning end against the wall, shaping it into a tiny glowing cone. "It was cracked and formal-sounding. She never spoke to me like that, before or after." He put his head back so that it rested partly on top of the wall and sighed.

"I went on up to their bedroom and pop was lying in bed, same as he'd been doing for the past couple days...but he was different."

Melanie didn't say anything. She waited.

"It was my pop but he was different. Like everything that actually *was* him — you know, all the stuff that made him who he was — like everything that made him who he really was had just up and left, leaving behind the body he wore." He took a drag on the cigarette and blew a couple of smoke rings.

"Anyway, seeing my mom so sad — I mean she was *devastated* when pop died — seeing her that way convinced me that relationships were bad—"

"What was that?"

"What?"

Melanie turned around, pulling her head down so that her eyes were level with the top of the wall. "I heard something."

Johnny stubbed out his cigarette and he too shuffled around so that he was looking over the wall. "Can't see anything."

Everything looked exactly the way it had been before. The clouds had left the moon uncovered and visibility was good. Johnny scanned the patches of road between the trees but couldn't see any movement. "They'll be well out of sight now," he said.

"No, it wasn't from the road," Melanie whispered. "It was nearer. Much nearer." She twisted onto her knees. "I'm going to go take a look."

"No." Johnny shot out his arm and took hold of Melanie's knee.

"What?"

"I don't think you should do that."

Melanie considered it for a few seconds. Then she said, "What does it matter if we're seen? If someone — some*thing* — is down there then we ought to know about it, don't you think?"

"Maybe it came from inside, downstairs someplace."

"Like what?"

Johnny shrugged. "I don't know what," he hissed. "Something falling over maybe?"

"Like what?"

"Will you stop with the 'like what'! I don't know *like what*...just *something*. There's a lot of stuff down there. Maybe it was a CD case slipping off a stack...something like that. Something completely innocent."

"And maybe it wasn't."

maybe it's the Lizard-man come to pay you a call, Johnny's secret head-friend whispered to him, *and he's brought various bits and pieces belonging to Geoff and Rick...dripping red pieces*

He shuffled the thought as far back as he could, out of sight.

"Shit, I'll look," he said, and he clambered up and leaned over the wall.

The concrete apron was deserted.

He scanned the grass and then looked across towards the bushes and trees that lined the driveway. Nobody there. No Lizard-men.

"All clear," he said.

Melanie scrabbled away from the wall. "I'll check inside."

Johnny thought about stopping her but decided against it. The station was secure — they'd spent long enough making sure that nobody but nobody could get inside unless someone let them in. He turned around, fighting back another thought: namely that he didn't want to go back into the station himself. And he hated himself for thinking such a thing...and then hated himself some more for letting Melanie go alone when, deep in the secret places inside his head, he feared that whatever she had heard it might not be a CD case falling off a stack.

He closed his eyes and stretched his neck back, feeling the tension ease a little. He heard a muffled grunt from the passageway and then a hissed 'Shit!' Almost immediately Melanie called out that she was okay. Then more mumbling. Johnny smiled to himself and waggled his head from side to side. The tension eased a little more.

He opened his eyes and stared across at the town road, scanning for any signs of movement. The tree tops looked still as paintings, shades of black against the deeper black that formed the woods at the far side of the road.

Johnny turned to the right and, slowly drooping his head, followed the road back, past the fork and all the way up to the concrete apron in front of the station. When the top of the wall in front of him appeared, Johnny moved his head slowly to the left, scanning the concrete.

Troy Vilawsky didn't register anything when Johnny's eyes met the Deputy's dark glasses. He just stood there, arms hanging by his side but each of them standing a little away from his body, like he was an old-time gunfighter, his head tilted back and seemingly watching Johnny.

Johnny felt exposed. He nodded, a sinking feeling

why the hell's he wearing dark glasses when it's pitch black?

starting off in the pit of his stomach and slowly

and what the hell's wrong with his arms?

working its way upwards like bile and

better still, when did he start wearing gloves, for crissakes?

threatening to explode into his mouth.

"Hey, Troy? How's it hanging?"

Troy didn't respond.

The Deputy had moved into Jesman's Bend a little over four years ago, transferred across from the coast, from some town nestled in the greater Los Angeles smog belt, for a break from the drug and gang warfare. *Some folks are made for that kind of shit, and some folks aren't*, Troy had told the folks in Martha McNeil's diner a couple of mornings after he'd moved in, his shirt pressed like a marine drill sergeant's. *Me, I'm made for things being a little quieter.*

It wasn't that Troy was slow in coming forward when he was needed, nossir. It was Troy pulled the man and woman from the blazing Subaru up on the mountain road that time, even went back a couple of times to get their little girl but she was long gone and the fire held him back. It was a blessing really: the girl had flown forward between the front seats and smashed into the windshield. Wasn't anything anyone could have done for her, not even Troy.

And it was Troy who tackled Jack Salliday when he'd had just a little too much tequila, and finally managed to get the serrated knife out of Jack's hand before Jack slit his wife's throat with it...Conchita Salliday having passed around just a few too many favors to the guys at the truck stop over on Boedecker Street down in Dawson. Conchita had taken a skillet to the back of Troy's head while her ever-loving husband had proceeded to slice open the Deputy's right side, the fleshy part just around from his belly. And Troy hadn't pressed charges that time, either, making sure instead that Jack Salliday straightened himself out some and stayed away from the booze and home more with his wife. *Might solve a lot of problems*, Troy had told Jack.

And now here he was, standing out in the night air wearing wrap-around dark glasses like he was a Hollywood heartthrob or something. He didn't look relaxed and he didn't look tense. He looked *wrong*. He just stood there glaring up — at least that's what Johnny figured he was doing behind those dark glasses: glaring.

Johnny shuffled his way to a crouched position, his knees against the wall, and he nodded towards town. "Everything okay, in town I mean?"

Still nothing, but now at least Troy turned around stiffly, like Jim in *Taxi*

town? whut's 'town' mean, man?
and looked in the direction Johnny had indicated.

As if on cue, Gram Kramer stepped out from behind a bush, ignoring the bush's branches scraping across his face. Gram's arms were hanging the same way as Troy's... awkward and lifeless. And he was wearing the same dark glasses, too.

Johnny glanced down at Gram's hands. Yep, the gloves were there.

All present and correct.

Johnny nodded. "Hey, Gram. How're *you* doing?"

Gram walked stiffly over to Troy and stopped. Troy turned around and joined Gram in looking up at the roof... at Johnny.

Johnny forced a slight laugh. Nope, things were most decidedly *not* okay in town. "Hey, come on guys...talk to me, will ya? At least tell me why you need to wear shades at four o'clock in the goddam morning." There was a noise from deep inside the station, deep down right underneath where Johnny was crouching.

Troy and Gram turned their attention to something right in front of them.

Johnny frowned: what *was* right in front of them?

He heard only the faint strains of Melanie's muffled voice but it was loud enough for him to figure out what she was shouting...shouting through the door, the door with the covered peephole that allowed folks inside the station to look out and see who was standing outside.

Hoo boy, she was shouting, or something like that.

And something like, *Am I glad to see you guys.*

Then Johnny heard Melanie shout out his own name, and he imagined the inevitable fumbling of her small and petite hands on the lock and bolt system that would undoubtedly follow...maybe was underway right now, even as Johnny struggled to his feet and made for the hatchway leading into the station.

Just hold on there, Melanie was probably saying as she fumbled, *and we'll have you inside in just a few seconds...*

As he plunged through the doorway into the blackness of the station's interior, Johnny didn't think that having Troy and Gram inside right now was a particularly good idea at all. Halfway along the corridor, when he heard a roll of loud thuds against the door, he had a sneaking suspicion that Troy and Gram didn't agree with him.

"Mel!" he shouted at the top of his voice, suddenly realizing how good it felt to make a loud noise. "Don't open the door!"

Twelve

"Back up, Geoff," Rick hissed. "For God's sake, back up right now."

"Jerry...?"

"It's not Jerry." Rick glanced down at the crowd in the town square. "It's not *any* of them."

The people were starting to amble — there was no other word for the movement they were making: they were ambling, a slow and formless motion forward — towards the grassy slope that led up to them. He turned around and saw that Jerry Borgesson was also ambling, thrusting one leg out in front of him, swinging it around like it was stiff or something, like he couldn't bend it at the knee anymore, and then, when the first foot had connected solidly with the ground, swinging the other in the same half-arc, his arms swinging by his sides. Then Jerry brought the arms up and held them out, the fingers flexing all the while like they were reaching for something.

"It *is* Jerry, for God's sake," Geoff said, his voice soft so that only Geoff himself could hear, in a tone that might just as easily have said, *No, it's not a lump...it must just be a bruise or something*, while he was inspecting his balls in the shower.

"Geoff, back up. Now!"

Rick was standing now, torn between retreating into the bushes and reaching out for his brother's arm. Jerry came on, stumbling a little, but apparently determined. Rick shot another glance down into the town square and saw that several folks were already making their way up the grassy hillside towards the road. None of them were speaking. Nobody was making any sound of exertion. There were no calls of *Let's get 'em, men!* or *What are those guys doing up there watching us!*...only a strange and silent relentless movement towards them.

Geoff stepped back and held out his hands. "Jerry, it's me...Geoff."

"Geoff, we have to get back to the station."

"Jerry, *talk* to me for crissakes."

The thing that looked like Jerry Borgesson finally pulled off his second glove and lifted his arms woodenly, without stopping its ambling movement towards Geoff.

"Geoff, we have to get back to Mel."

Cynthia Crasznow's head appeared to the side of the road, her arm reaching out a gloved hand to grasp at tufts of weed and branches in an effort to pull herself up another few feet. She keeled over to one side, no expression on her face, and lay there for a few seconds, waving her arms and legs like a turtle that had been turned over on its back. Then she managed to right herself and shifted around to get a better grip. She was wearing the same dark glasses as Jerry Borgesson. And the same gloves, dark and skin-tight, but thick...making her hands look out of proportion to the rest of her body.

Over behind the filling station a throaty roar let out, too guttural for a regular sedan. Whatever was making the noise, a truly anguished belly-ache of a noise, was bigger than any regular automobile.

"Geoff..."

Geoff turned around and looked at his brother. The look said everything that Rick felt. It held a deep sadness and an almost primal fear. The sadness was for the world, that had suddenly seemed to go all to hell. And the fear was of something that was completely unknown and unfathomable.

Jerry dropped one glove to the ground. The second one followed almost immediately. Then the arms stretched out again, reaching for Geoff's back.

Without stopping to think, Rick leapt forward, stumbling on a tuft and completely losing balance, pinwheeling his arms like he was going to take off and fly up into the night. A sharp pain hit Rick's side and he rolled over, grunting in pain. As he started to pull himself to his feet, Rick saw Geoff start to turn.

But it was a micro-second too late.

Rick watched as Jerry Borgesson's hands took hold of his brother's head, one hand at each side, holding it almost tenderly, like it was an over-ripe pumpkin that Jerry didn't want to squeeze too hard.

As Cynthia Crasznow lifted to her full height and started tugging at her own gloves, pushing her feet one in front of the other through the thick grass, and as Gram

Kramer's pick-up tow truck appeared over Main Street and began a slow slide over to the left, towards the radio station, Geoff Grisham threw his arms forward and opened his eyes and mouth wide.

"Riiiiiii—"

Rick got to his knees and looked around. He found a thick gnarled branch and lifted it with both hands, lurching forward in a variation on Chuck Berry's famed duck-walk and, pulling himself upright at the last second, took a swing that would have shamed Yogi Berra. The branch hit Jerry Borgesson on the side of his head and Geoff could have sworn he heard something crack. As Rick's arms reached their full extent, he drew the branch back into view, fully expecting to find it had shattered. But it was still whole. The crack had been something else, something from inside Jerry Borgesson's head, but whatever it had been didn't seem to be causing Jerry any problems.

Jerry continued to hold Geoff's head, and Geoff's eyes rolled upwards, showing white. His entire body was shaking, like he had his fingers jammed into a wall-socket, soaking up a few thousand volts.

Rick took another swing, this time catching Jerry full in the face, and jumped sideways, shoulder-charging his brother. Jerry stumbled backwards, his face suddenly dark and wet, letting go of Geoff's head but his arms still stretched out. Geoff slumped to the ground like a sack of potatoes.

But the damage was done.

Geoff's right eye slid back into view and Rick saw it catch his own.

In that brief instant, Rick felt as though he was looking into his brother's soul. The expression told him to get away, to get away as fast as he could, and to look after Geoff's wife and keep her safe. But there was also pain in there, a lot of pain. Rick could feel it in his own head, could feel it shriveling his insides, turning them to mush. Then the expression faded and, as though on auto-pilot, Geoff shuffled around on the floor, trying to get up.

Rick didn't think there was any real understanding in Geoff's mind at that point, just a simple reflex mechanism. He'd heard of it before, read about it in books about the war in Vietnam, people fatally wounded pulling their exposed intestines together and trying to stuff them back through their ruined shirts and into their stomach or bending down to retrieve limbs blown off by mortar shells or land-mines.

He'd seen a bird doing the very same thing one time, back in the house in Providence when he was just a kid. A cat had got the bird, a big white cat that he had used to like stroking and listening to it purr. The cat had torn off one of the bird's wings and gouged a big chunk out of the side of its face, just next to the tiny beak. For what seemed like an age, the bird had shuffled around on the spot — watched quietly by the cat lying right next to it on the lawn — lifting its one good wing and trying to flap the exposed muscle of the other...just going through the motions as it tried to get back to normal, slumping as its legs kept giving way first to one side and then the other. Meanwhile, all of the bird's systems were mercifully closing down.

Rick figured that his brother's systems were being closed down in exactly the same way, the little men inside his body turning off all the power, all the screens, watching them go blank and flat-lining one by one.

Then Geoff's eye plopped out onto his cheek like the crazy glasses you could buy in joke stores, and a thick dark substance oozed out after it. He lifted a hand to his face and patted the gunk gently, then shuddered. He moved his hand away and rested it on the ground, seemingly trying to get his breath.

As Rick watched, Cynthia Crasznow stumbled towards him, closing the ten yards that separated them.

Meanwhile, Jerry Borgesson shuffled into a sitting position. The dark glasses were gone, knocked off into the long grass. He started to lever himself up onto his knees, one arm waving around in front of him as though he was blind, the fingers on the hand constantly grasping.

Geoff projectile-vomited over his own legs, a long string of something solid-looking hanging from his mouth. He paused for a second, ignoring what was dangling from his mouth — and still bubbling in waves — while he patted his face again, sticking a finger patterned with leaf and grass shards into the empty eye socket. He suddenly shuddered uncontrollably and his other eye dropped onto his lap. More ooze followed and Geoff slowly lay back on the ground.

Ed Donahue stepped from around a thick tree trunk, having climbed up from the road. Next to Ed were little Janie Sullivan and Marcy Culpepper, two blonde girls of around ten years old that Melanie had said would be breaking a lot of hearts in just a few short years. All of them were wearing dark glasses...and gloves, although Marcy and Ed were already beginning to remove them.

Rick got to his feet and swung the branch at Cynthia Crasznow, catching her in the chest on the second attempt. Cynthia faltered, took an involuntary step backwards and

then lifted her foot to move forward again. Rick brought the branch down on the top of the woman's head and brought her to her knees. One final blow sent her face forward onto the grass.

He took a final look at his brother, the vomit still pulsing from his mouth like a well...and it was vomit that no man had any right throwing up. It didn't look like the usual stuff — carrots, corn kernels, that sort of thing, all held together in a gelatinous brown wash. This vomit looked like stuff that a man really couldn't afford to be without...gray, concertinaed tubing and tubular valves dripping with viscous, all of it steaming as it lay on Geoff's chest.

Rick turned around in time to see Jerry get to his feet. His eyes narrowed and, swinging his club-branch behind his head, he took two steps and brought it round into the side of Jerry's head. The head snapped sideways and flopped over, the ear torn off and a chasm opened up from Jerry's jawbone right to his eyebrow. Even as Jerry was falling, the branch came down one more, this time in the opposite direction, and caught Jerry full in the face. He went back and down, and didn't move.

Marcy Culpepper had managed to remove her gloves and was daintily stepping around Geoff to get to Rick, her arms outstretched.

Behind her came Ed Donahue and Janie, and behind them came other shadowy figures just appearing over the rise, all of them wearing dark glasses, all of their faces expressionless, and all of their arms held out in front of them. Rick felt a wave of panic when he saw that a lot of them had already removed their gloves.

He turned and plunged into the thick bushes and branches, heading away from town and the road that led back to the station. There was a ravine somewhere up ahead, and the trees got so thick it wouldn't be possible for a man to break through them...at least not without a lot of effort. Rick was confident that he would have the energy when the need arose but he wasn't too sure about the time it would take to do the job.

But somewhere in the back of his head, he knew the first thing was to head directly away from town and the road that he would eventually need to take. The road was exposed, that was the first thing. And Rick was very aware of the cars and trucks that the townsfolk already had in the air, maybe patrolling the open land. Here in the dense woodland he was safe from that at least.

But the road held other dangers. The townsfolk may already be making their way back that way on foot, breaking off up the hillside to the forest path in little splinter groups, their arms outstretched before them.

Branches tore at him, scratching his face and tearing his shirt, and he had the old familiar feeling of something coming up behind him, reaching out for him. This time, however, it wasn't the two cyclists he had run down. This time it was something altogether different.

Every few steps, he tried to move to his right, aiming to travel in a wide circle that would eventually bring him out onto the bridge road that led back to the station. He heard himself moaning and couldn't stop it. Then the tears came and he re-played Geoff's death in his mind. "Stop it, stop it for crissakes!" he shouted, wiping snot from his nose and mouth with the back of his hand. "Got to keep moving," he said, "got to keep heading forward and right, forward and right...that'll do it. That'll be okay." But he wasn't too sure.

He burst through a waist-high bank of gorse, grimacing as the thorns raked his thighs, and plunged head first down a steep incline. He closed his eyes and tried to turn himself around, swinging out with his right hand to grasp something...anything. But the only things there to grasp were far too busy tearing his clothes and his flesh.

He bounced against trees, thankfully only glancing them, and was repeatedly spun around and over, lashed by branches and hit by rocks that tumbled after him. He eventually came to a halt in a narrow gully along which water trickled soundlessly. He waited, half-expecting to set off again, and opened his eyes. Miraculously, he didn't seem to have broken anything though both legs and his right arm felt almost numb with constant small collisions and, whenever he tried to move, a thick stabbing pain flashed across his lower back.

"Got to...got to keep my head clear," Rick whispered to the night. "Got to get back to the station."

He spat dirt and leaves and sat up, moaning when his back complained. He leaned forward and twisted his left arm around to rub the small of his back...and to feel for protruding bones. There weren't any and, after a couple of minutes, his breathing became more regular. The image of his brother's eyeball plopping out flashed into his mind. He screwed his eyes shut, fighting back the tears, and leaned his head against his knees while he searched inside himself for strength.

A rustle from somewhere nearby made him look up.

Where normally he might have said, in a soft voice, *Geoff?* he had to bite his tongue. Geoff wasn't coming.

Christ, Geoff was dead. What the hell was Mel going to say? How was he going to break it to her?

The noise came again, somewhere over to the left. It sounded too small to be a person. And anyway, he figured it was in the wrong direction for it to be one of the townsfolk...or whatever they were now. Paradoxically, of course, it was the other direction — the one from which the townsfolk *might* be coming, all gloves and dark glasses — that he now needed to go.

The rustle came again and something small scurried across a piece of open ground to his left before disappearing into a thick clump of bushes.

The sound of a motor drifted into earshot and Rick looked up at the canopy of trees, delighted to see that the covering was so thick nobody had any chance to see him.

It was surprisingly light down here, with the real darkness beginning only three or four layers of trees in any direction. He took a deep breath and considered his plan.

In order to get back to the station he had to go right, to follow the gully. If the gully veered off to the left, away from the station, then it must eventually hit the bridge road or at least run within sight of it. And morning couldn't be too far away now — he grimaced involuntarily at the thought: it was already morning, with only the light still yet to appear. He looked at his left wrist and saw a thick welt where his watch strap usually sat. He must have lost it on the way down.

He looked up again in the hope that maybe he would see the first tell-tale signs of sunrise but there was only a dark sky overlaid with silhouettes of branches. That and the sound of a distant motor, quickly joined by a second...like a pair of dogs growling in annoyance that their prey had gone to ground.

He leaned over to his right, resting his weak arm, and levered himself to a kneeling position. It was uncomfortable but not impossible. He pulled his left leg so that the foot was on the ground and pulled himself upright by holding onto a long branch that swept the ground from high up. The branch rustled like a reluctant horse letting its passenger know it had some reservations about carrying him, but eventually he was standing on both feet, albeit crouched over like an old man and shaking at the knees. He let go of the branch and straightened up, waiting for a stab of pain. The stab didn't come.

Rick lifted each leg in turn and rubbed the calf muscles and the ankle, feeling for strains or lumps. Everything seemed to be intact. With a quick look around, he unzipped his pants and took a pee. The sound of the water pooling on the ground was familiar and reassuring. He zipped up, took a deep breath and moved off, carefully at first and then speeding up as he grew used to the terrain. He tried to concentrate on keeping his breathing even and deep, filling his lungs and breathing out, building his stamina and his reserve. Never mind whoever or whatever he might encounter on the way: he would need everything he could muster when the time came for him to face Melanie.

Thirteen

Johnny smacked his head against one of the high cupboards, the one with the door that wouldn't close properly. Everyone in the station knew it didn't close properly but the advantage they usually had was that they could see the damned thing hanging out there, right at head height. Rick had been promising to fit a new magnetic catch switch on it but, like so many little things, it hadn't been done.

He rubbed his head and cursed.

"Damned thing could've put my fucking eye out."

Thuuuum! Thuuuum!

More thuds echoed through the station. The visitors were getting impatient.

Mel's voice chimed in and Johnny could hear it now. "Just hold your horses for a second will you?" That meant two things: one was that he was closing the distance and the other was that Mel hadn't yet managed to shift the deadbolt.

He reached across and ran his hand along the wall until he found the light switch and flicked it. The overhead tubes sprang to life, their light flickering on in stages and humming. The hum sounded good.

Johnny reached the end of the corridor and opened the door.

Thuuuum! Thuuuum!

The thuds were louder now and it sounded for all the world as though they were already inside, big feet stomping up the stairs towards him.

"Mel?"

He flicked on the switch for the staircase and started down.

"Yeah? Ah...this goddam bolt!"

"Mel, don't open the door."

There was a pause. "What?"

He rounded the bend in the stairs and started down to the ground floor, taking them two at a time. The darkness ahead looked threatening.

"I said—"

Thuuuum! Thuuuum!

"Jesus Christ, what's the *matter* with those guys! *Will you*—"

"Mel, don't open the fucking door!"

Johnny skidded into the corridor alongside the spare studio downstairs and hit the light switch. As he ran past the studio window he glanced in. Everything looked so normal in there: stacks of CDs — even though the studio had not been used for more than a year — playing decks, microphone. What the hell had happened to the world, and how had it happened in so short a time? Maybe they were all going to wake—

Thuuuum! Thuuuum! Thuuuum!

Then again, maybe they weren't.

He pulled the door open at the end of the corridor and came face to face with Melanie. She was standing between the door that led into the garage and the main door, frowning. Johnny saw fear in her eyes.

He glanced at the bolt and saw that it was almost clear of the housing and her hand was still on it. He stopped and looked at her, raised his arms. "Mel, don't open the door." He felt the indescribable and completely incomprehensible urge to laugh.

Thuuuum! Thuuuum!

"Why not?"

He was ten maybe fifteen yards away from her. If she decided to pull the bolt — he couldn't see whether the key had already been turned but he suspected that it had — then he may not get to her in time.

"Mel, trust me on this, okay?"

"Johnny, you're...you're frightening me."

He took a step forward.

Thuuuum! Thuuuum!

"Mel, I don't mean to frighten you—"

the hell you don't, a tiny voice said in the back of Johnny's head, *you* mean *to scare her* shitless...*cos if she opens that fucking door you've got a whole heap of trouble, compadre, and you can take that to the bank*

"—but I don't think we should open the door until we figure out what they want. That's all I'm saying."

"What they *want*! Jesus Christ, Johnny—" Melanie pulled the bolt and it slipped out of the housing. "—it's Gram and Troy..."

Thuuuum! Thuuuum! the barrage sounded, as though to confirm.

"... *Gram and Troy!*" She nodded to the door. "*Listen* to them! What the hell's the matter with you?"

Melanie reached down to the key as Johnny gave a shrug and walked quickly towards her. *Hey, okay, you're right*, the shrug said. *What is the matter with me.. gee, I dunno, maybe I'm coming down with an attack of anxiety.*

Melanie's face softened when she saw Johnny's apparent resignation. She shook her head, muttering, and turned the key.

Thuuuum!

Johnny leapt forward.

Melanie let go of the key and started to turn the handle.

Thuuuum!

"Mel! Get out—"

The throaty growl of an engine slowly grew outside but it sounded like it was coming from above...like a helicopter maybe.

of the way!"

Melanie started to turn in shock, letting go of the door handle.

Thuuuum! Thuuu—

But the door was already ajar.

Silence settled on the scene and it settled awkwardly.

Johnny stopped dead, watching the open door and expecting to see it burst fully open...expecting to see Gram and Troy standing there, looking like a cross between the

Blues Brothers and a couple of Herman Munster lookalikes, complete with axes and chainsaws.

Melanie looked at the door and then at Johnny, her initial smile faltering a little. "What?"

Johnny waved for her to move back.

Melanie did as she was told but repeated her question. "*What?*"

Outside, the helicopter was beginning to sound as though it was about to land on the roof.

"What the hell is the matter with you?" Melanie shouted to be heard over the noise. She jerked a finger upwards. "Hear that? We're gonna be rescued and you're behaving paranoid."

Johnny took a faltering step forward and then another.

Maybe he *was* being paranoid. Maybe the guys in town had decided to give them an early Halloween scare, making out they were pod people or something.

yeah, and maybe you'll win the lottery next week and there's something in your genes that'll mean you live till you're a thousand, the small voice said in Johnny's head, *but don't take* that *to the bank*

Two more steps took him right up to the door.

Holding his arms straight out, and flattening his hands against the door, he stooped to look out of the peephole.

As he looked, the noise of the engine changed into a thundering crash of splintered stone, fractured metal and breaking glass, coming from directly overhead.

Melanie screamed as dust and fragments of plaster showered down on them. But Johnny didn't turn around. He was too busy looking into the face of Troy Vilawsky. He was standing right up against the other side of the door, pulling off his gloves. Johnny couldn't see Troy's eyes — the dark glasses were still firmly in place...flashy-looking things, wrap-around with strange markings — but he knew

here come de Lizard man, the small voice whispered, *and he mighty pissed at all this work he's had to do just to get inside to meet you*

that it wasn't the Troy Vilawsky he'd known these past years. Aside from the gut feeling that he had, Troy's face was smashed and bleeding, his shirt stained black...as though someone had pounded his head with a bar

or maybe he been pounding his head on something else, the voice chuckled, *like the door, f'rinstance*

"But the glasses..." Johnny said softly. "They're not even scratched."

"Johnny!"

From upstairs came the sound of things falling over.

Johnny started to push the door forward as gently as he could.

Then, from just to Troy's side, Gram Kramer stepped into view, his arm held out in front of him. Gram's lower jaw was hanging down, the teeth broken and the gums dripping blood. Gram's arm was heading for the gap in the doorway.

Pushing as hard as he could, Johnny shouted, "Mel, get out of the way."

A gloved hand snaked through the gap and around the door, the fingers grasping.

The door hit Gram's arm close to the elbow. Johnny leaned to the side and looked through the peephole. Gram was reaching up with his free hand, holding it palm out ready to push. He didn't seem to be in any pain.

Melanie screamed again.

Something crashed upstairs, something in the corridor leading to the staircase, and fresh clouds of dust fell around them.

Johnny took hold of the door handle and, with his other hand primed to push, he pulled the door off Gram's arm, waited a second until the arm fell a little — it didn't seem to be visibly damaged but only one of the fingers was still grasping, and grasping feebly. Then he pushed with all of his might.

The door knocked the arm back out of sight and hit firmly into the jamb.

He turned the key. And slid the deadbolt home.

Outside, something crashed to the ground from upstairs.

Thuuuum! Thuuuum! Thuuuum! Thuuuum!

Melanie was crying. "Johnny...what's happ—"

A crash of breaking glass from upstairs drowned out her question.

Thuuuum! Thuuuum!

Johnny looked out of the peephole and saw Gram and Troy calmly smashing their heads against the door. Pieces of bone and tissue flecked their shirts and hung from their faces, but the expressions showed no pain or fear or anger or even intent. There was just nothing there at all. He turned around and took hold of Melanie's shoulders.

"Mel, we have to get out."

Thuuuum! Thuuuum!

Melanie looked up at him, her face a mask of terror. All she could think of to say was, "Where's Geoff?"

"Mel—"

Thuuuum! Thuuuum!

"Johnnyohjohnnyjohnnyjohnny." She gulped in air. "Where's Geoff? I'm so frightened. Geoffgeoffgeoffgeoffgeoffgeoff—" As she wailed, saliva flecked her anguished mouth in thin strands, the words merging into and even becoming each other, so that her cry was more a mantra of grief and regret and fear than the simple question it had set out to pose. "—geoffgeoffgeo—"

Johnny slapped her hard across the face and, momentarily silenced, she slipped from the grasp of his left hand, sagging to her hands and knees on the floor, where she began to sob.

Thuuuum! Thuuuum!

"Mel."

Johnny looked down the corridor to where the stairs led upstairs — or, more importantly, to where the stairs led down from upstairs — half-expecting to see feet descending slowly towards them.

Thuuuum! Thuuuum!

"Mel," he said, as softly as he could, crouching down in front of her and gently taking hold of her shoulder. "First off, I think that the helicopter or whatever it was has crashed into the station. *Numero deux*, they're inside...and I don't think they're here to rescue us." He held up three fingers in front of her face. "And three, we have to get the hell out of here pronto, *capice*?"

Mel continued to sob and Johnny took a look around.

There was a single *Thuuuum!* on the door and then silence, broken only by a solitary rattle of some small object falling to the floor upstairs.

Melanie looked up and wiped her eyes. "He's dead, isn't he?"

"We don't know that, Mel."

She nodded, her eyes blinking their confidence. "I know it, Johnny. I can *feel* it...can feel it *here*." She placed a hand on her left breast.

Johnny didn't say anything.

Melanie looked across at the door. "It's stopped. The noise."

He nodded.

"I think I preferred it to the silence." She shook her head and ran her fingers through her hair. "Who are they, Johnny? What do they want?"

"I don't know. I'm pretty sure they're not who they appear to be — not the folks from town." He thought of Troy and Gram beating their heads to a pulp on the door...and managing not to get a single mark on their sunglasses.

Johnny waited a few seconds and then said, "We have to leave the station."

"What if he comes back and we're not here?"

Johnny ignored the fact that Melanie had referred only to Geoff and bit the bullet. "If he's...if *they're* dead, then they won't be coming back," he said. "That's...that's just a simple fact, Mel. But if they are *not* dead — and we don't know that they are — then we don't want for Geoff to have to come back to you being dead. Are you following me here, Melvin?"

She sat back on the floor with her back against the wall and, just for a second, a tiny smile tugged at her mouth the way it always did whenever Johnny called her 'Melvin'. She nodded and wiped her cheeks and eyes with her hands. "Yes, I'm following you."

He took hold of her hands in his own and pulled Melanie to her feet.

"Okay. We need to get the keys to the Dodge — you know where they are?"

"Shit! Did Geoff take them?"

"Why would Geoff take the keys?"

"I don't know. I don't know that he did. I just—"

She looked up the corridor towards the stairs.

"Did you hear that? I thought I heard something."

"Don't worry about that — I'm keeping an ear open for anyone coming down. I think they're busy checking the place out...the studio. And they don't seem to move too fast."

Melanie considered asking what made him say that and thought better of it. "Who put the car away?"

"You or Geoff. I didn't do it, and that leaves only you two."

"Geoff did it. You know, I think they might be in the ignition?"

Johnny shook his head at the questioning lilt of Melanie's statement. "Thinking isn't enough, Mel. We need to have the keys before we go into the garage. Once we're in there, the only way we're coming out—"

aside from maybe coming out in the Lizard Men's lunch boxes, he thought with an involuntary shudder

"—is in the Dodge. I don't want to get in there and find I have to sneak back into the station for the fucking car keys — pardon my French."

Johnny raised his hand and shook his head as Melanie was about to speak.

The shuffling sound upstairs had stopped and had been replaced by a constant but strangely gentle and hypnotic droning noise, which seemed to be getting louder. Then the noise turned into a *plunk, plunkplunk—*

They both looked across at the stairs

—plunk, plunkplunk—

and watched as Geoff's lucky baseball came into view

—plunkplunkplunk, plunk—

tumbling carelessly down towards them, missing stairs occasionally, before

—plunk, plunk, plunkplunk....

reaching the corridor in front of them and rolling gently to a halt by the side of the bureau standing against the wall just a few yards away.

"The decision's made for us," Johnny whispered, nodding to the garage door. "We'll chance to luck that the keys are in the ignition."

"And if they're not?"

Johnny shrugged. "Then we're up shit creek without a paddle."

The shuffling had started again, moving along the corridor above, a cumbersome sound apparently without much coordination. Johnny tried not to think about who — or what

it's the Lizard Men

— might be making that awkward movement...and just why the movement should sound quite so difficult.

"Hey, I've got an idea."

"What?"

Johnny trotted across to the big bureau standing against the wall next to Geoff's lucky baseball. He took hold of the bureau sides and was delighted when he discovered it was on casters: the thing not only moved easily but soundlessly as well. "The garage door opens inwards," Johnny said as he pulled the bureau along. We'll stand this right in front of the door and hope it takes them a little time before they figure out where we are."

Melanie frowned. "You're making them sound like first-graders," she said.

"Well," Johnny said, puffing as he maneuvered the bureau into place, "it took Geoff's baseball for them to hit on the concept of going down the stairs."

As if on cue, a loud clump rattled on the stairs, followed by another. Then, at the same time, another clump and then another.

"Three of them," Johnny said.

Several more clumps sounded.

Melanie shook her head. "More."

Johnny nodded.

Melanie turned the key in the door to the garage and pushed it open. Then she helped Johnny pull the bureau into place behind them, before gently closing the door again. Just as the door closed and the last vestiges of light faded, Melanie saw shadows coming down the staircase at the end of the corridor. She slipped the key into the lock on the garage side of the door and turned it quietly. The darkness felt good. Safe.

"The bulb is gone in here," Melanie whispered.

She sensed Johnny nodding, sensed his head pressed against the door listening for sounds from the corridor beyond.

"We won't need light to get into the car and we'll get all we need once we're outside."

Melanie felt a thick column of ice-water begin around her shoulder-blades and travel quickly down the full length of her spine. "Johnny..."

"Mmm?"

"We don't have the remote for the door."

Something in the station, on the other side of the door, had come across Geoff's lucky baseball. His ear pressed against the wood, Johnny listened to it rolling and rolling, rolling and rolling until, at last, it clunked loudly against the door.

Which meant it had rolled under the bureau.

Which might also mean that whoever or whatever had kicked or knocked the ball had seen it. And had possibly seen where it went. And had possibly noticed, above the bureau, the unmistakable outline of a door in the wall.

Johnny hoped that wasn't significant.

Fourteen

Rick had made slow progress along the gully before branching off to the right up a wide avenue between the trees, as though someone — a long time ago, because the avenue was grassed and heavily cambered — had been considering creating a spur to the road down into Jesman's Bend.

That might have made sense: it would have meant a direct route straight into Dawson, creating a dog's leg with the Bend right on the knee-joint. But then maybe it was something else entirely, such as a simple track once used by natives of the area or loggers perhaps.

The track kept narrow for a long time and Rick was nervous about how close the trees were as he passed them. Close enough to touch in some places...or for something to reach out a hand — an ungloved hand — to touch *him*. Or maybe one of the rag dolls he'd left on the road through the mountains all that time ago — seemed like another lifetime — stepping out from behind the tree and *hey, asshole, whyn't you come back and finish the job... think there's a couple of bones here seem to be still in one piece*

giving him a piece of their mind.

Once or twice he thought he saw shapes moving behind the trees, but they were squat shapes and not even remotely human-like...unless the townsfolk had taken to moving around on all-fours, which Rick didn't think was necessarily as unlikely as it sounded.

And there were constant engine noises passing overhead though after a while, particularly as he started to move up towards the road again, the noises seemed to be further back. He presumed the townsfolk — or whatever they were now — were still busy patrolling the lower woods for signs of him. After all, they must surely think that anyone in his or her right mind would not head back to civilization, particularly after the events overlooking the town. And maybe that was his ace in the hole.

Rick wiped his nose and squinted into the gloom.

The trees seemed to be thinning out up ahead, sufficiently so for him to make out a space in the distance which gave onto more trees. That space could simply be a clearing, of course. But it could also be the road.

the big question here, audience, is a two-parter: first part, for ten points — what part of the road, or even which road, is it? and for tonight's star prize, who or what else is watching it?

Rick walked slowly and stealthily, picking his steps carefully amidst the twigs and bracken. Eventually, he saw that it was indeed a road. He sat down and settled into a cross-legged position, pulling his wet and torn trousers so that they were not touching his leg, and waited.

A dark shape passed overhead, purring softly in a hovering position before banking off to its right across the trees at the other side of the road. Rick couldn't tell what the vehicle was nor could he understand how the occupants could see anything — the car (if it *was* a car) was displaying no lights nor any search beams. A thought struggled to express itself, as though this discovery were in some way significant, but another engine noise caused Rick to flop back prone amidst the trees and the thought — something to do with the absence of light — faded away for a few moments.

When he was satisfied that the engine had moved off, Rick dismissed the thought completely and stood up. He stepped carefully down the slight bank and onto the road.

The pavement felt good under his feet...felt right.

He looked to the right and saw the road bend around, sloping downhill. To Rick's left it went pretty straight and always gently uphill. He'd come back onto the Jesman's Bend road and he had mixed feelings about that. On the one hand it made things a lot easier; on the other, it made him feel more vulnerable. Rick didn't think there would be much, if any, traffic from the Bend on the road that went straight out from the station and over the bridge. But this one could be different.

He turned around, checking the treetops for the amount of cover they provided and considered moving back into the woods and making his way through the trees. Each way had its advantages and disadvantages. The bottom line was weighing speed against safety...bearing in mind that being safe wasn't much help if it delayed him to such an extent that everyone in the station was dead by the time he got there.

Clearly a balance between the two was called for.

He decided that he would move along the road, keeping a close eye on the woods so that he could duck into the trees at the first sign — visible or audible — of anyone coming along.

"Well, what is it they say about every great journey starting with but a single step?" Rick whispered to the night.

He was answered with a distant hum coming up from the right. Head down, he ran across the road, dived into the bushes — narrowly missing a thick trunk that had been sawn off at around waist height — and rolled beneath swaying fern fronds and bush branches. Holding his breath and not daring to move, he looked between the leaves.

It seemed like only seconds later — so quickly, in fact, that Rick was sure he must have been spotted — that Daryl Engstrom's 1970 tomato-red Plymouth 'Cuda came up the road. Rick knew it was the 'Cuda even though he couldn't make out the color — Daryl's cheesy swinging furry dice hanging from the rear-view kind of gave it away. But it wasn't Daryl driving. In fact, Rick couldn't make out who it was but the car was full...three men and one woman it looked like, the woman's hair long and tied back in a pony-tail.

The three men — one of whom was driving — seemed to be looking straight ahead. The woman, sitting in the front passenger seat, was staring out of the window in what appeared to be a contradictory mixture of intent and disinterest...but, just for a second as the car drifted by, her dark glasses faced directly towards Rick's position and he felt the eyes behind those black frames boring into him. He ducked down further, setting a branch to swaying right above where he was hidden.

It was Jennifer Bacquirez, one of the Bend's most eligible spinsters: as he crouched, heart beating, Rick idly wondered whether spinsters could be said to be eligible in the same way that bachelors could. For the briefest instant, it seemed an important consideration...and he yearned for the times, so recently ended, when such thoughts were worthwhile. And then the instant was gone.

Rick waited for the car to stop or turn around and head back to his hiding place...but it didn't. The sound of the engine grew fainter until it was gone and the silence flooded in again.

He waited, then raised his head.

The road was deserted again. They hadn't seemed to be looking for him.

Rick got onto his knees and then stood up, shaking from head to foot.

Suddenly, it made sense.

It was the road down into town, which also meant that it was the road heading out to the station. And Daryl Engstrom and his friends *weren't* looking for him...they were heading specifically for the station.

Heading for Melanie and Johnny.

Without another thought, he trotted down onto the pavement, glanced back once and then set off. He would be there in five or maybe ten minutes. And in another few yards, when he rounded the next bend in the road, he could cut across over the old fence, drop down through the trees and come up on the station from a position of cover.

Ten minutes maximum.

He hoped that would be fast enough...and tried hard not to think about exactly what he was supposed to do when he got there.

Fifteen

"Now what?"

"Now," Johnny whispered, matter-of-factly, "we get in the car and see if the keys are in the ignition."

Melanie nodded. "Good plan, Captain."

"It's always good to have a good plan."

"They're the best kind."

"Uh huh."

"Johnny?"

"Yeah?"

"Are you scared?"

Johnny couldn't stop the smile. "Constipation seems like a luxury right now. Like, mightily desirable."

He moved silently and slowly along the side of the Dodge to the driver's door and took hold of the handle.

"Can you see them, the keys?"

He turned around from trying to stare through the window. "Can you see me, Mel?"

"Nope. I can tell where you are, but I can't actually see you."

"Right. So how do you think I can see the fucking keys inside the car, in the ignition, hidden behind the steering wheel?" He hoped she hadn't realized that he was actually pressed against the glass trying to find out for himself.

"Sorry."

"No, *I'm* sorry. I didn't mean to snap."

"S'okay."

"I have to open the door."

"Well, we always knew we'd have to do that."

"True. But now that it's come to it, I can't help wondering whether we should just sit tight and hope that everyone goes."

Melanie's voice sounded disconsolate in the darkness of the garage. "Not much chance of that, I fear."

"I fear your fear is well-founded, Lady Melvin," Johnny agreed.

And he pulled the handle.

The Dodge's interior light glimmered until he pulled the door fully open, and then it shone as bright as a lighthouse beacon. He leaned on the seat and shuffled his shoulders across.

"The keys are here."

Melanie threw back her head and thanked whatever gods were in charge of giving suckers an occasional even break.

Johnny shuffled around a little. Melanie heard the glove compartment open and close, and then things being moved around in the small recess which straddled the transmission — sunglasses, packs of gum, pens. She knew what he was looking for.

"Is it there?"

Johnny backed out of the car and closed the door gently. The darkness was immediate and absolute. He pulled it ajar again and the light returned, quelling the sudden flurry of panic in Melanie's chest.

"Can't see it if it is." He stood up and moved back to where Melanie was standing. "Where would he put it?"

She shrugged and then said, "Christ, it's anyone's guess."

"Here? In the garage?" She looked around at the clutter of forgotten and stored items hanging from the center beam or propped against the walls.

"I...I wouldn't have thought so."

Johnny let out a deep sigh.

"Sorry."

Johnny looked into her eyes and smiled. "It'll be okay."

"Will it?" she asked pleadingly.

He let the question hang and said, "I have to go back."

"Into the station?"

"What else can I do?"

"Can't we...can't we ram the door?"

"Oh, sure...but it won't give. It might, after a few dozen attempts — assuming we don't damage something under the hood, or chew the wheel arches up so's they ride on the tires."

He walked to a chest of drawers standing in the corner and rummaged about in the cans and glasses of paint, each one boasting an abandoned brush standing to attention, its bristles long ago hardened. "The thing is, what'll they be doing while we're doing that?"

"Well, we have to—"

It was an easy thing to do. And normally, it wouldn't have mattered.

But, of course, this time it did.

Johnny was reaching for what looked like a piece of plastic that could have been the remote control for the door mechanism.

But it wasn't.

And nor was the goofy-looking cross-eyed reindeer standing on the shelf below, the shelf against which Johnny's flapping shirt sleeve brushed. The forgotten Christmas decoration slid drunkenly to one side, Johnny's eyes widening as he saw what was happening and—

"Johnny!"

—it lurched fully over, rolled the few inches to the shelf's edge and, even as Johnny shot out his free hand, dropped.

Johnny's hand missed, hit a can of Dulux gloss paint that Geoff had used to paint the sills outside the studio a couple springs ago, which in turn knocked over a bottle.

The reindeer hit the floor with hardly a sound.

The bottle didn't.

Johnny cringed at the sound of breaking glass and the additional, almost musical

hey viewers, what sounds like a bell and smells like shit?

duuh-uuh-uuhung! as it bounced first onto the metal tub containing cloths and a vicious-looking tangle of old clothes that Geoff and Melanie had either grown out of or which had been left behind by the fickle whims of fashion...and then onto the floor.

The silence which followed that seemingly endless reverberation was pure and, in and of itself, a noise all of its own. And it was perhaps *that* noise — the calm that trailed in the wake of the storm — that drew the most attention.

"Shit!" Melanie said.

It was a lot more appropriate than some idiotic question like, *D'you think they heard?* Particularly as that question was answered almost immediately.

Thuuuum! Thuuuum!

"Shitshitshitshi—"

"Shh," Johnny hissed. "If we can't get out, then they can't get in. The garage door's metal, for crissakes."

And then somebody started to move the bureau from the station door behind them.

"That one isn't," Melanie said without a single trace of emotion.

Sixteen

The first thing Rick noticed was the trunk of Daryl Engstrom's 1970 tomato-red Plymouth 'Cuda hanging out of the upper floor of the station. If the situation had not been so difficult, the scene might have been comical, the car stuck onto the building's roof like a huge boil or an unsightly canker on the side of a favorite tree.

Rick had come up on the station from the woods, with the building taking shape from the top down behind the trees, etched against the steadily lightening eastern sky like an apocalyptic drawing sketched perhaps after the very same tornado that had taken Dorothy and Toto from the safety of Kansas to the harsh landscape of Oz had hit 21st Century Jesman's Bend and the immediate area.

He sidled his way between trees and bushes, being careful to avoid disturbing the foliage. As the concrete-aproned entrance and the adjoining garage door came into view he was glad of his stealth.

There were about half a dozen of them shuffling around at the main doorway into the station.

Two more — one of whom was Troy and the other Rick didn't...no, it was Gram Kramer — were wandering across to the garage door. Troy seemed to have been in some kind of accident...Gram, too, he saw. It was clear even from where Rick crouched that the heads and shirt fronts of Jesman's Bend's favorite deputy and gas jockey were covered in blood. Had there been some kind of fight? And if so, had it happened in town or here at the station? Rick feared that the latter was the most likely — he couldn't imagine the townsfolk beating each other up, and certainly not to the extent that Troy had been beaten.

A loud creak sounded from above the throng and Rick looked up in time to see Jennifer Bacquirez push open the 'Cuda's warped door and start to get out of the car. He felt a sudden urge to shout and tell her

hey, Jenny, don't do that!

that the particular section of Daryl Engstrom's pride and joy she was struggling to exit was suspended some 15 feet or more above solid concrete. Nobody else seemed to be paying any attention.

In fact, Troy was now apparently concentrating on the garage door, his head tilted to one side. He was listening for something.

A dull thudding crack snapped out as Jennifer Bacquirez fell to the concrete. Nobody turned around.

Gram Kramer wandered over to stand beside Troy and the pair of them started banging their heads

Thuuuum! Thuuuum!

against the garage door.

Now Rick understood where the blood had come from. He looked across at the station door and saw the dark stains — he knew what those stains were.

Gram lifted his arms and slammed them against the garage door, thrust his head forward and rammed it. Troy did the same.

On the concrete apron, the prone figure of Jennifer Bacquirez struggled to right herself. She was lying on her back, one leg doubled up beneath her and the other one — her left — thrashing up and down. She looked for all the world like an upturned insect trying to turn itself over.

Rick watched others from the group wander across to the garage where Troy and Gram had built up an obtuse rhythm. Sally Pennington and Grace Sheffield joined them and commenced to provide a counter-beat. Nobody was saying anything — stranger still, nobody was screaming at the pain they were inflicting upon themselves. The same went for the smashed Jennifer Bacquirez, who still flapped her arms and single leg from the concrete, groping around for some means of support. She was still wearing her dark glasses. And her gloves.

Rick glanced around at each member of the group. All had on their dark glasses and all were wearing gloves.

Now there were four of them banging away at the garage door with various parts of their anatomy. One thing above all else was starting to worry Rick: and that was the fact that, slowly and surely, their movement seemed to be improving.

Back at the spot where he and Geoff had been watching the people from town, their coordination had been more stilted. What he was watching now was still a far cry from complete coordination, but it was drastically improved and more fluid. Rick didn't think that was a good sign.

A loud crash sounded from inside the station.

Troy and Gram stopped their beating and tilted their heads until two more crashes rang out. Then they re-commenced.

More crashes came from inside the garage. The activity could mean only one thing: Johnny and Melanie were inside the garage. The trick was how to get them out.

Then there was a loud shout and the sound of things falling and breaking, and a high-pitched scream which turned into Johnny's name. That was followed by more smashing.

A single clunk from the garage door stopped Troy and Gram and their activity once again, this time inspiring them to stagger backwards and stare at the door. It had moved. That meant that Johnny and Mel—

Rick looked across to his left and saw Jennifer Bacquirez holding something in the air. She had shuffled her way around so that she now lay on her side.

Sally Pennington and Grace Sheffield turned around and looked at Jennifer without Jennifer having said anything. Troy looked as well, and Gram. Jennifer moved the object in her hand towards her until she was holding it right in front of her glasses. She shook the thing, shook it harder, then tapped it — surprisingly gently — on the concrete. Then she switched hands, like a baby trying to figure out how her favorite toy worked, and

clunk, rackerrackerrack—

the door moved again.

Sammy Lescombe emerged soundlessly from the bushes over to Rick's right. Everyone turned to face him without Sammy having said anything. He was carrying an armful of thick branches which he proceeded to hand out to the people at the garage door. Now Gram walked up to the door and, with what appeared to be superhuman effort, brought his arm back and swung his branch — a thick piece of tree bole — forward to crash against the door. It made a loud reverberation. There was a shrill scream from the other side of the door, followed by a chorus of crashes.

Troy followed Gram's example with his own stick.

Jennifer took hold of the object in both hands, held it steady and

clunk, rackerrackerrackerrackerracker—

pressed.

The garage door was moving upwards.

Troy and Gram, Sally, Grace and Sammy shuffled forward, holding their branches menacingly.

It was now or never.

Rick burst from the bushes and headed for Jennifer and the remote.

Abby Buchanan stepped from the shadows of the station doorway even before Rick was onto the concrete, striding her legs by swinging them out and forward...like the knees were locked and wouldn't bend. She lifted her arms out in front of her and started pulling off her gloves.

On the floor, Jennifer Bacquerez stopped waving her arm around and turned her head to face in Rick's direction. Rick noticed that the banging on the garage door had stopped.

He reached where Jennifer was lying and stopped to glance back at the garage door. Troy had moved away from the door and was walking in Rick's direction. His movements seemed a little stiff but generally okay... certainly a lot better than the movements Rick had seen back at the clearing just a couple of hours ago.

Troy hefted his branch and did a trial swing with it. There looked to be a lot of power in those arms, and Rick didn't want to be anywhere near.

Gram stepped over near the door and just stood there like a sentry on guard duty, his own branch resting in his arms like it was a rifle. Sally, Grace and Sammy fanned out into a horseshoe configuration making it so there was no way Rick could get to the garage door without encountering at least one of them. Sally removed her gloves and dropped them onto the floor. Grace did the same.

When Rick looked back he saw that Jennifer had pulled off one of her own gloves and was reaching the bare hand out towards Rick's leg. He kicked at the hand, felt it connect and watched her arm fly backwards behind her head. It was only a momentary retreat, though. Meanwhile, Abby Buchanan was shuffling her way to cover Jennifer's back.

Rick looked down and saw that Jennifer had switched the remote into her other hand, the one whose arm was pinned beneath her. She was holding the remote close to her chest — Rick saw the swell of her breasts, the slight point on the nipples, and realized that Jennifer was not wearing a brassiere. In any other circumstances, such a revelation would have prompted other thoughts, a drying up of saliva... maybe even an exploratory movement from behind his trouser zipper. But now it didn't do diddly. He pulled back his foot again and kicked Jennifer in the face. Rick didn't pause to check the damage he had done — Jennifer had rolled over fully onto her back and old Abby was getting too close for comfort. He bent down, retrieved the remote which was now held very loosely, and turned around...just in time to see Troy making his swing.

How the hell had he gotten over here so fast?

Rick dodged backwards and sidestepped towards the bushes.

Troy swung his branch — Rick heard it funneling the wind right in front of him — and adjusted his direction.

Abby had stopped to help pull Jennifer to her feet but as soon as she moved away the temporarily erected siren of Jesman's Bend slipped sideways on her ruined right leg and landed back on the ground. Abby paid her no more heed.

Rick looked across at the garage door, back to the side at the steadily-advancing Abby, and then at Troy. There was nothing else for it. He needed something — anything — that he could use as a weapon and the only thing he could see was Troy's branch.

He slipped the remote in his trouser pocket and made like he was going to tackle Troy. The deputy swung the branch but Rick had already stopped. As the branch flew by, Rick jumped forward and slammed into Troy's belly, his head tucked down so that it crunched into the deputy's chest.

They both flailed backwards a couple of steps and fell onto the floor before Troy could get his branch back in action.

Abby adjusted her direction and shifted around.

Sally and Sammy started forward from the garage door.

Rick pulled at the branch but Troy held it up over his head with one arm. He wrapped the other around Rick's back.

The hold was like a vice. Rick couldn't move. And there was the strangest smell coming from the deputy...a staleness, like old clothes that needed a wash or flowers that had been left too long in a vase whose water had evaporated in the heat.

Rick tried to push himself up but couldn't break Troy's hold.

Eventually, his left hand hit something solid amidst the cold shirt. Troy's holster. And in Troy's holster was—

Rick pulled the gun and jammed it into the deputy's side.

Abby was now just a few yards away.

In the other direction, Sammy and Sally were holding out their arms expectantly, stumbling forward, reaching for him.

Rick tried to pull the trigger but it wouldn't move.

Safety catch!

He snuggled in tighter to Troy's belly so that he could get his other hand around to the gun. If only he knew something about these things but he didn't. He arched his back, trying to make his middle narrower so that Troy's bone-crushing hold wouldn't be so intense.

Melanie's voice screamed from the garage...Johnny's name.

Rick found the catch on the gun, fumbled with it until it moved and then pushed it all the way.

Something dropped in the garage, echoing in the gloom.

Rick pulled the trigger.

A muffled explosion cut through the early-morning air.

Troy lurched and, from somewhere deep inside of the deputy's stomach, Rick heard a groan.

The hold relaxed, but only a little.

Sammy and Sally were now only a few yards away, their hands bare and clawing at the air greedily.

Rick pushed and the arm loosened still more. He pulled his arm from the side of Troy's belly and held the gun with both hands, pointing the barrel into the deputy's gut. "This is for Geoff," he whispered. The gun exploded and threw him backwards.

Something brushed his shoulder as he bounced back onto the ground. Right in front of him, old Abby was bent over reaching down to where he had been. He lifted the gun with both hands again, and fired into the old woman's back. She lurched forward, arms outstretched, and landed on top of Troy.

Rick rolled over and jumped to his feet. He looked down at the gun — three shots. He had fired three shots — which meant, how many were left? Three? Was it a six-shooter? He felt like an old-time gunfighter.

Over to his right, Sammy Lescombe moved to one side, covering Rick in case he ran wide back to the safety of the trees.

Sally Pennington widened her arms like she was about to try taking off.

Rick lifted the gun and fired at her.

The shot went wide.

He staggered forward, holding onto his back with his left hand, and held the gun as steady as he could in front of him. He pulled the trigger and Sally lifted from her feet and hit the ground skidding.

Rick started to run, the remote suddenly in his left hand, the gun still held in his right, heading for the garage door and for Grace Sheffield, standing with her arms held out to greet him.

Sally rolled over onto her side and tried to stand up. Blood was streaming down the front of her dress, running down the folds and onto her legs.

Sammy Lescombe turned around and started to close the gap between himself and Rick.

"Melanie!" Rick screamed. "I'm coming!"

Seventeen

The muted shuffling around the door leading back into the station was suddenly replaced by a loud crash.

"Oh, wonderful!" Johnny said. "They know we're in here."

There were two more crashes.

"And they're not using their hands," Melanie added. "They're trying to smash it down with something."

Johnny pulled open the Dodge's door so that they had some light. He pointed to one of the four inlaid wooden panels: it had splintered, a thick shard of wood bellying out at a right angle to the door. "And they're doing a good job."

"What do we do?"

"Fight for it?"

"How?"

Johnny walked across to the door and took hold of the key. "We open the door and—"

Another crash drowned out his words.

"And we charge them."

"We don't know how many there are out there."

Johnny nodded. He looked back at the car and then at the door.

Crash! Crash!

When he looked back at the door into the station, he saw the unshaven face of Daryl Engstrom peering through a wide crack in the left hand panel. The face pulled back and another crash took out the panel completely, the wood flying past Melanie's head and bouncing against the Dodge's trunk.

"There's not much choice," he said. "There's no way out through the garage door, not without the remote. Got to do it before they have a chance to think about it."

Johnny breathed in deeply, smiling at Melanie's outstretched hand as she grabbed his arm. Melanie loosened her grip and patted his arm.

Johnny took hold of the key and turned it gently, making sure there was no noise. Then, with his hand on the handle, he pulled the door wide open.

There were three of them, Daryl Engstrom at the front with Jimmy James Poskett and little Elsie Weebershand flanking him. The most striking thing about them — aside from the fact that they were all holding either pieces of broken chair or, in Daryl's case, the metal hat-stand christened 'Bullwinkle' by Rick — was the entire lack of anything even resembling personality on their faces.

Daryl's stubbly chin was thrust before him in a manner of confrontation but there was no other sign of aggression, though Rick couldn't see his eyes. The thin-lipped mouth was clamped shut — even though Daryl should have been surprised, shocked even, by Johnny's sudden appearance — and Daryl's hair, a thick thatch of wheat that was graying slightly around the ears, was unkempt and hanging over his forehead.

"Daryl, what's goin—"

Jesman's Bend's brawny odd-job cut off the pleading question with a two-handed swipe of the hat-stand into Johnny's shoulder that sent him staggering backwards through the doorway. Daryl swung the hat-stand back and stepped forward. Elsie Weebershand, fourteen years old and, Johnny knew, sporting silver braces behind that cold and tight-lipped half-smile, sidled through at the same time, brandishing what the dazed Johnny quickly recognized as a chair leg from the studio. The leg came down on Johnny's shin and he heard rather than felt a dull crack: the pain came a few seconds later, washing up his leg like flood water.

Melanie grabbed a shovel from the wall, dislodging a metal watering can which rattled onto the floor nearly deafening her. She leapt forward as the small girl, very small for her years, was pulling back for another swipe. The metal end of the shovel struck Elsie full in the chest, momentarily pinning her against the door jamb before Melanie's forward momentum sent her back through the doorway. Melanie swung around and hit Daryl in the cheek but it was only a glancing blow. Daryl hefted the hat-stand forward, an over-the-head thrust like he was hammering stakes into the ground. The hat-stand hit the top of the doorway and he lost his grip with one hand which flew forward clenched into a half-fist.

Johnny groaned from the floor. "Oh, Jesus Christ!"

From somewhere behind them — maybe in another county or an alternative universe, Melanie thought — the familiar clunk of the garage door opening joined the confusion and then stopped.

Melanie tried to ignore the fact that

oh, great, now they're coming in behind *us*.

the garage door was opening. She swung the shovel back and slapped it onto the top of Daryl's head but it barely caught his skull and, instead, raked the side of his head and thudded ineffectively on the big man's shoulder. When she pulled the shovel back to try again, Melanie saw that Daryl's right ear was partly severed, blood dripping down the side of his head onto his pale blue collarless shirt.

As Daryl staggered, losing hold of the hat-stand which clattered to the floor, Jimmy James Poskett powered through and swung Geoff's baseball bat, the tip connecting with Melanie's elbow and continuing until it reached little Elsie Weebershand's face. Blood and bits of what could only be bone — plus Elsie's teeth — skittered across the floor and sprayed the door jamb and a cabinet containing screws and nails, all in neat little jars, which Geoff kept just inside the garage. Elsie dropped her chair leg and fell backwards, arms pinwheeling, until she hit the floor.

Melanie jabbed the shovel forward, grunting, and smiled when it sank into Jimmy James's neck. The shovel moved him back, pushing Daryl back fully into the station even as he tried to reach the hat-stand. Melanie pulled back and jabbed forward again, the curve of the shovel lodging itself in Jimmy James's eyes snapping the intricate and expensive-looking shades. The glasses fell to the floor and Jimmy James dropped the baseball bat and threw up his hands...trying to cover his eyes, but catching a shard of thick, black glass that was lodged at the bridge of his nose and pushing it deep into the left socket.

Melanie closed her own eyes and held back the bile.

The garage door started to move again.

She spun around. "Johnny...the door!"

"I-I know," Johnny grunted. "Can't move. My leg..."

Melanie turned back and, grunting, swung the shovel at Daryl who was pushing his way into the garage. The shovel caught him fully in the stomach. The big man staggered backwards, turning in an attempt to remain upright, and fell over the crouched figure of Jimmy James — still fumbling with his ruined eye socket — who, in turn, tottered over the prone body of little Elsie Weebershand.

There was a loud *crack*, like a car backfiring...and someone was screaming but Melanie ignored the noise, only distantly aware in another part of herself that it was coming from her own mouth.

She stepped forward and brought the shovel down on the back of Daryl's head...lifted it, and swung it across and at an angle, catching the back of Daryl's neck. The blade of the shovel dug into the flash and jarred on the spinal column. Daryl's dark glasses tumbled from his face onto the floor and, although seemingly oblivious to the damage, exposed tendons and cartilage in his neck, he lifted his hands to his face even as it connected with the floor.

From behind her came another *crack*, but it wasn't a car backfiring. She knew that now. It was a gunshot. Then another. And another.

She shifted the shovel to her right hand and picked up her husband's baseball bat with the left. Then she dropped the shovel and hefted the bat in both hands. It felt good. It had been a long time since she and Geoff had played softball but it was coming back to her. She took a few practice swings, keeping an eye on the trio twitching on the floor in front of her. Daryl lifted himself up and turned his head towards her, and blinked.

The two red blobs where pupil and iris should be were not like anything she had ever seen before...at least nothing that didn't appear in a movie theater. Daryl shifted himself to one side, with no grunt or sign of exertion, and he started to pull off one of his gloves. Jimmy James lay where he had fallen, moving his head from side to side. Little Elsie Weebershand didn't appear to be moving at all.

"Mel..."

Ignoring Johnny's call she took an image of exactly where Daryl's head was, closed her eyes and swung the bat as hard as she could. In her imagination, she heard a pumpkin split open, pieces of it hitting the corridor walls. Seconds later came the unmistakable sound of something falling to the floor. She turned around and opened her eyes.

Johnny was pointing at the door.

"I know...it moved. I heard it. Gunshots. The cavalry must be on its way." She moved over to where Johnny lay on the floor next to the Dodge and crouched down beside him. "You okay?"

He shook his head. "Leg...hurts like hell."

"Can you move?"

He laughed without humor. "Well, there's no way I'm staying here."

"Melanie!" a voice screamed from outside. "I'm coming!"

The door started to move upwards.

Melanie turned to watch it, a smile breaking out on her face. She ran to the door, holding her hands on the metal as it slid upwards. "Geoff? Geoff, I'm okay."

Outside the garage, Rick stopped dead in his tracks.

Melanie's voice...he'd heard it. But she was shouting for Geoff. How was he going to tell her? Grace Sheffield ambled from side to side, moving her legs up and down like pistons, her gloves on the floor by her feet. She raised her arms and opened them towards him.

Over to Rick's right, Sammy Lescombe was still moving forward with just a few yards to cover before those welcoming arms and hands would reach him.

Rick tilted his head and listened to the wind. There was a sound on it...no, more than one sound — there were *several* sounds riding the breeze. Engines.

He looked up and saw the sky lightening to the east.

He looked back at the road that wound down first to the bridge and then on into town. Engines were coming but they weren't coming up the road. He lifted his head and watched the tree tops. They were coming up there.

There wasn't much time.

Rick turned to Sammy Lescombe — the same Sammy Lescombe that he'd bought provisions from and talked baseball statistics and chewed the fat about the weather — steadied his hands and aimed for his chest. The bullet took off the right side of Sammy's head, his dark glasses with it. Sammy shuddered, took a step or two back, and then three wavering steps to the side, his right leg buckling as though about to give way. Then he fell forward, stiff as a board, arms still outstretched, and didn't move.

Rick stepped forward and picked up Sammy's branch, hefted it to test the weight. Then he turned to face Grace... Grace Sheffield with her powder-white hair and her delicately-patterned dress of fine cotton, wafting around her legs.

"Grace...back up now," Rick shouted. He slipped the gun into his pants pocket and waved the branch with his right hand. "I don't want to use this but I will if I have to. Now just let me by."

He trained the remote at the garage and pressed.

The door moved upwards, clanking.

The sound of engines was getting louder.

Melanie emerged from beneath the door, a baseball bat in her hands. She looked left and right and then across at Rick.

Rick saw the smile falter a little and then return, but when it returned it was a false smile. "Geoff?" She craned her head to look behind Rick and took a step forward, following Grace who still doggedly closed the gap between herself and Rick. "Where's Geoff?"

Rick sighed, both at the fact that he was going to have to deal with Grace and the fact that he was going to have to deal with Melanie. He wasn't sure which one he was looking forward to the least.

"Rick, where's Geoff?"

"Back up, Grace," Rick snapped. "I mean it."

"Rick!"

"He didn't make it, Mel." He waited for a few seconds, watched Melanie's face take on a quizzical expression. *Didn't make it? What kind of shit was that?*

"How do you—"

"He's dead, Mel. Geoff's dead."

Melanie dropped the bat.

Grace staggered another couple of steps...just a few feet away now. Rick shook his head. He waited for her to take another step, braced himself and swung the branch, clipping the side of her head and knocking the dark glasses across the concrete. Grace staggered, partially bent forward, and then straightened up. When she turned to look at him she lifted her hands to her face...but not before Rick saw the woman's eyes. They looked like coals, hot coals, red and black. She rubbed her face, swiveled around, clawing at her eyes.

"Grace..."

Melanie had retrieved the bat. She walked calmly forward until she was standing in front of Grace Sheffield. Then she brought the bat down on top of the woman's head with all of her might. Even with the sound of the engines, Rick could hear her sobbing. Melanie lifted her arms back behind her head to take another swing but Grace had fallen face forward, a thick black pool forming beneath her head.

"Mel, she's finished."

As Melanie brought the bat down and pulverized the back of Grace's head, Jack DiChapperlain's Camaro appeared over the trees. Behind the Camaro was Suzie Mendohlson's open-sided Jeep, with Roy Clubb hanging out of the passenger side. There was something in Roy's hand.

A loud report echoed and a thick cloud of brick and dust exploded from the side of the station.

Rick dived forward, dropping the branch, and grabbed Melanie.

"Shit, now they've got firepower."

Another shot rang out but Rick didn't see where it went.

"Inside," he shouted over the roar of the engines. Another one was coming up from the bridge road but Rick wasn't about to waste time by turning around to see what it was.

Melanie was sobbing, the bat still clutched in her hands, repeating Geoff's name over and over again.

Roy Clubb's rifle snapped at the night again and a piece of masonry bounced inches from Rick's foot as he dragged Melanie across to the garage, all but throwing her inside.

"Where's Johnny?"

"GeoffGeoffGeoff...oh my *god*...he *can't* be—"

Rick slapped her and grabbed her shoulders before she could fall over.

Craaack!

One of the old paintcans leapt into the air, bounced against the Dodge's windshield and rolled down the hood.

"Over here," Johnny said, his voice weak.

Rick pulled open the Dodge's left-hand back door and pushed Melanie inside. He slammed the door and edged his way around to the back of the car to where Johnny was laid out, barely conscious.

"What is it? Bullet?" He searched Johnny's shirt-front for signs of blood. "Knife?"

Johnny shook his head. "Broke my leg. Daryl—"

"Doesn't matter who did it, Johnny." He looked around. One of the cars was landing — he could see dust billowing up just outside the garage door.

Craaaack!

Melanie screamed.

When Rick looked through the back window he saw the windshield was a mosaic of tiny lines.

"Shit," Rick said. "We have to move."

Another shot rang out, followed by another.

"Rick...I don't think I'm gonna be—"

"I know. I'm gonna have to do it."

Rick lifted Johnny by the armpits and dragged him around to the other side of the car. He pulled open the door and dropped him onto the back seat, cracking Johnny's head on the door-surround and wincing as Johnny screamed out in pain when he lifted Johnny's twisted leg and jammed it into the footwell so he could close the door.

Rick pulled open the front passenger door and fell in, dragging himself across the seats and the center panel. He was shaking as he slipped into the driver's seat and rested his feet on the pedals.

A loud *crummmmp!* came from somewhere up above and a thin cloud of dust drifted down onto the windshield and the back window. Johnny leaned forward and looked up through the windshield.

"Something's landed on the roof," he said. It sounded so casual and

hey, some pod people have souped up a whole bunch of the townsfolks' autos so's they can fly...and they've landed one of them on the garage roof

matter-of-fact, and Rick didn't feel that way at all. Mostly, he felt tired.

Outside the garage door, Martha McNeil's rusted old Chevy flatbed did a shaky three-point landing, with Martha at the wheel and Frank and Eleanor Dawson crouched down in the back. Frank and Ellie were over the sides of the Chevy even before Martha had turned off the engine, and Frank was carrying a shotgun.

He shouldered the piece and brought it steady, letting off the barrels one at a time, taking a thick chunk of masonry and wood out of the top left of the garage door frame, and doing some damage to the Dodge's grill. Rick felt the car jolt and hoped it was only lights that had caught the blast.

"I don't care," Melanie was saying between tears. "I don't care about anything...I don't—"

"Shut up, Mel," Rick snapped. Then, "Johnny, I don't know as I can do this."

Johnny shuffled himself into an upright position and faced forward. "Sure you—" He broke off and winced at the stabbing pain that shot up his thigh. "Sure you can. Just like riding a bike — you never forget."

Frank and Ellie Dawson were striding across the concrete towards the garage, Ellie dragging a long-handled ax along behind her and Frank busy trying to load cartridges into his 12-bore.

Rick turned the ignition and

just like riding a bike

felt the Dodge thrum into life. He placed his hands at ten before two on the wheel, gritted his teeth, shifted the gear lever into **Drive** and

you never forget

looked outside.

Frank and Ellie Dawson had gone. In their place were the shimmering memories of two bedraggled figures, covered in blood, thick slices of flesh hanging from them. One of them — the girl...couldn't have been more than twenty-two, twenty-three — was wearing cut-off blue denims and

she had freckles, didn't she Rick? you remember that, don'tcha...you remember seeing her face in that much detail just before

the guy was lifting something up...

"Rick—"

like he was waving

hey, asshole, whyn't you come back and finish the job... think there's a couple of bones here seem to be still in one piece

to him but no...he was holding something out towards him...

"Rick! For Christ's sake...he's gonna—"

Johnny's voice broke the spell.

Melanie screamed and Rick felt her head come forward into the back of his seat.

In front of the car, Frank Dawson was clipping the stock into place.

Jim Ferumern walked stiff-legged around the garage door, coming out of nowhere, his gun in his hand. He let off a shot.

Somewhere behind them, in the garage, something gave a thin *thunk!* and whined.

Now out of the flatbed's cab, Martha McNeil walked jauntily up behind Frank like she was going to tell him something...let him into a secret.

"*Rick, drive the fucking car!*"

Ellie Dawson reached the hood and brought her ax down into the windshield. The Plexiglas buckled.

Johnny leaned forward and pressed the door catch, listening with relief as all four of the Dodge's doors locked.

In a daze, Rick released the parking brake.

Jim Ferumern lifted his gun and tried to train it. Frank did the same with his 12-bore.

Martha McNeil came up behind Frank and brushed his shoulder, Frank shifting the 12-bore just a fraction to the right as he pulled the trigger for the first barrel, the shot taking off the top of Ellie's head, even as Ellie was hauling back with her ax. She stopped for a second, staggered a little, and then continued to heft the ax.

"*Drive* for crying—"

Rick stepped on the gas and the Dodge leapt forward, spinning Ellie Dawson around and smacking her into a run of shelving...pots and cans and drill-bits spilling onto her and onto the side of the car.

Johnny shouted out in pain as he leaned to the side, resting his head on Melanie's hip.

The Dodge hit Frank in the crotch, doubling him over, the 12-bore skittering across the hood to the windshield and then rolling off of the driver's side.

Frank held on as the car screeched out of the garage, side-swiping Martha's flatbed, the wheels spinning, burning rubber.

Jim Ferumern stood watching, apparently taking everything in, his gun still trained, his eyes unseen behind the dark glasses, holding the gun level with the side windows.

Melanie screamed again.

Jim got off a shot. It went wild.

Rick braked, watching Frank slide forward off the hood.

In the rear-view, Rick saw Jim training the gun again... saw Ellie, the top of her head gone and no hair at all, saw her heft the ax and stagger out of the garage. He floored the gas pedal just as Frank slid off the hood, felt the car bump — twice — over the body

hey, you're getting real good at this kind of thing, Rick

as they spun around on the concrete apron.

Overhead, another car was circling — Rick didn't know what it was.

He heard shots, heard a dull *thunnnng!* on the roof, and aimed the car for Jack DiChapperlain's Camaro which was parked outside the station door, all four doors wide open.

Rick took one of the doors clean off, felt the Dodge judder, and bent the other one on that side back flat against the front side-panel.

Roy Clubb stood up from behind the Camaro. He was holding a rifle.

Something went *ziiiinnng* across the hood and Rick spun the wheel, fanning the Dodge's rear end just as Suzie Mendohlson climbed up from the woods — glancing down, Rick caught sight of Suzie's open-sided Jeep, lying in the trees on its side. The Dodge hit her legs and sent Suzie up into the air and back down to rejoin her car.

Rick checked the rear-view.

There were two cars on the garage roof!

Ellie was lying on the floor.

Jim was walking after them, the gun hanging by his side. Then Roy appeared in the mirror, the rifle held slack. Neither of them appeared to be in any rush.

you heard another engine, didn't you drive-boy

Rick hammered the gas and spun the wheel to head for the road. As he turned the corner, he saw Jack DiChapperlain waiting for them.

Jack was standing in front of a battered blue-and-white, the furry tail on the antenna telling Rick it was Don Patterson's. The car was parked right across the road. Jack pulled his rifle up into sight and fired.

Rick lurched to one side and the shot hit the windshield.

hey, drive-boy...whyn't you fire back?

He reached into his pocket, pulled out Sammy Lescombe's gun. He slammed the brakes and knocked out the buckled Plexiglas just as Jack was preparing for another shot.

Rick held the gun as steady as he could and pulled the trigger.

The shot went wild.

"Rick!"

Jack tilted his head and lifted the rifle.

Rick fired again.

Jack staggered, a red patch spreading around his gut. He looked down at himself, regained his balance, and lifted the rifle again.

Rick pulled the trigger.

Nothing happened.

"Hit the fucker!" Johnny screamed from the back seat.

Rick stomped on the gas and drove. He was suddenly aware he was screaming...and Johnny was screaming...and now Melanie, she was screaming too.

The Dodge caught Jack DiChapperlain and carried him the three or four yards to the blue-and-white and squashed him like a bug. Rick lurched forward, his head colliding with the rear-view and swiveling it out of place, just as Jack slumped forward onto the hood. The blue-and-white hadn't moved.

Rick adjusted the rear-view and checked the road behind. It looked crowded.

Now, alongside or slightly behind Frank Dawson, came Daryl Engstrom — carrying what looked like the old hat-stand from the station — J. J. Poskett, some kid whose name Rick couldn't remember, Shirley Pakard and three or four more people...Eddie from the sheriff's office, Luke Napier, Janey from the deli, and someone else that Rick didn't recognize. They looked for all the world like The Wild Bunch or The Dirty Dozen, walking down the road with the station in the background, various articles in their hands. Frank raised his shotgun and let off a shot. It didn't connect with anything.

Rick faced forward and stared at the blue-and-white.

Then he glanced up at the rear-view.

He shifted the lever into **Reverse** and hit the gas.

"What the *fuck*..."

"No choice, amigo," Rick said to Johnny, half turned around in his seat, his arm resting on the back of the empty passenger seat alongside him. "Got to build up some speed if we're gonna move the patrol car." He gave a little shrug.

The Dodge careened back up the road, the townsfolk growing bigger through the back window.

Melanie shook her head. "You think you can do it?"

Rick didn't answer. He hit the brake about ten or twelve feet away from Frank Dawson, and shifted into forward gear again.

"Do or die," Rick said as they started forward again.

Someone fired a shot but it went wide.

"Amen to that," Johnny said.

Melanie patted Rick's shoulder and braced herself against his seat-back.

Rick aimed the Dodge at the blue-and-white's hood, where the least weight was. "Hold on!" he shouted.

Jack DiChapperlain's body was still twitching when the Dodge hit it, jerked a foot or so into the air, and sent the blue-and-white's front end spinning. The Dodge was almost by before the blue-and-white's trunk jack-knifed around from the other direction and hit their trunk, sending the Dodge's wheels spinning dangerously close to the edge of the grass which fell away sharply on the left down to the woods. But Rick kept control, twisting the steering wheel first one way and then the other, the wind blowing in his face through the smashed windshield.

They lurched down the road until they came to the bridge and the left fork down into Jesman's Bend. Rick brought the Dodge to a halt.

"Where to?" Melanie asked.

Rick shook his head.

They all turned around and looked back up the road. The sun's rays were clear from behind the station, a bright glow of hope.

"Oh oh," Rick said, a cold knot in his gut.

"Oh no," Melanie said.

The familiar sight of Martha McNeil's Chevy rose up, swaying side to side in the first touch of dawn's light...and then veered off towards town.

"They're— they're not coming after us," Johnny said.

Rick watched as the Jeep rose up and followed the Chevy. "Doesn't look like it." He shielded his eyes against the still watery light, and thought of all the dark glasses the townsfolk were wearing...even at night.

He turned back to face front and leaned forward looking up into the sky. It was blue now...still a murky blue with shades of night mixed in, but the blackness had gone. He pressed down on the gas.

"The Interstate," he said.

Johnny tried to straighten his leg and yelped. "Then where?"

"Then we need to find others...we need to find out what's happening, why it's happening and what we can do about it."

By the time they pulled onto the Interstate, the sun was coming up on a world that was both empty and, aside from the occasional car and truck smashed through the central barrier or upturned on the grass at the side of the road, deserted.

"You know," Rick said into the wind buffeting his face, "I'd forgotten just how much I like driving."

Epilogue

It was after seven o'clock when Rick finally decided it was safe to stop.

Rick waited until he saw a car that he liked the look of and then pulled in.

But, each time, the car had been damaged, running into metal fence-posts or outcroppings of rock, and the ignitions had all been left on and the batteries were stone dead. Rick decided they would have to wait until they hit a stop somewhere and, sure enough, one came up.

The place appeared to be called, somewhat unimaginatively, **Diner**, and the car was a shiny blue Cadillac Seville, a late '70s model that had clearly been cherished by its owner, he or she having moved on to the same place everyone else had gone.

It was parked alongside four 18-wheelers, a little foreign job with a stick-shift, and a couple of rust-buckets, all sitting outside a coffee house about fifty miles outside of Cheyenne. Four sets of keys had been on the counter, sitting beside half-eaten plates of food or newspapers open to the sports pages. The process of elimination had identified the ones that belonged to the Seville, a fob which also contained house keys for an unknown home and a bendy Bugs Bunny figurine.

The place was deserted and, after clearing the counter of greasy plates and cups of cold coffee, Melanie made them fresh coffee, poured orange juice, and put together a plate of sandwiches and stale Danishes while Rick checked over the Seville for gas and oil.

They had strapped up Johnny's leg as best they could and pumped him up with painkillers from a machine on the wall, but the pills were really only meant for headaches brought on by driving, not for broken shin-bones and they were having only a limited effect.

Nobody said much at all.

They used the washrooms to freshen up and ate in silence, each of them lost in their own thoughts and Melanie spending most of the time turning the dial on an old radio set on the shelf behind the counter. All she got was static. When it got to nine o'clock, Rick said that it was time to be moving on.

The Seville's dashboard clock registered 9:08 as they pulled out onto the road again, heading south.

The sun was blistering.

The sky was a pure blue unbroken by clouds.

And the road stretched off into the distance.

They didn't know quite where they were heading but Melanie and Geoff had honeymooned in the Rockies, when they had developed a liking for the Mile-High City, and Melanie had expressed a desire to go visit again. Rick and

Johnny had shrugged together at that: hell, one place was as good as another, though they all felt that they needed a big city to try to come to terms with what had happened.

Up ahead, down the long miles that lay before them, a telephone was ringing in the concourse of the 16th Street Mall in the deserted city of Denver...the very same way it had been ringing, off and on, for the past couple of days.

But it would be some time before they would be able to hear it.

And even more time before they got a few answers instead of just more questions.

To be continued in:

WINDOWS OF THE SOUL
FOREVER TWILIGHT: BOOK TWO